REX STOUT

O9-BHJ-489

Too Many Clients

*Introduction
by Malcolm Forbes, Jr.*

BANTAM BOOKS

NEW YORK • TORONTO • LONDON • SYDNEY • AUCKLAND

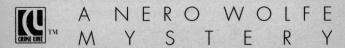

A NERO WOLFE
MYSTERY

This book is fiction. No resemblance is intended
between any character herein and any person,
living or dead; any such resemblance is
purely coincidental.

TOO MANY CLIENTS

A Bantam Crime Line Book / published by arrangement with
The Viking Press, Inc.

PUBLISHING HISTORY

Viking edition published October 1960
Bantam edition published March 1962
Bantam reissue edition / April 1994

ISBN 0-553-25423-5

Published simultaneously in the United States and Canada

PRINTED IN THE UNITED STATES OF AMERICA

OPM   15 14 13 12 11 10 9 8 7

Introduction

We are entering an era when the already considerable appeal of Rex Stout's Nero Wolfe mysteries will grow exponentially. This new age is symbolized by the microchip, which is extending the reach of the human brain the way machines extended the reach of human muscle during the industrial revolution. We will be reminded as never before that the source of all wealth and progress is the human brain, not material things. This has always been true, but the microchip will make it so plain that even the most obtuse will have to acknowledge it.

In ages past, wealth was thought to lay in material things: armies, gold, jewels, land, and, until a little over a century ago, slaves. You can't touch and feel software the way you can a slab of steel or a bar of silver. Yet in the hands of daring entrepreneurs these pieces of plastic can create riches beyond the imaginings of even the greediest Croesus. They enabled a poor southerner, Sam Walton, to storm and humble the seemingly impregnable corporate fortresses of Sears, K Mart, and others. The secret of Wal-Mart's success was using sophisticated inventory software that enabled it to respond immediately to marketplace changes and to simplify magnificently the layers of middlemen between stores and suppliers.

The information age will change our lives as dramatically as did the machine age. This era is emasculating centralized bureaucracies, giving unprecedented powers to countless millions of individuals. It will also make possible a cultural renaissance. The coarsening of American life over the past half-century will begin to be reversed. With high-definition, interactive television on countless thousands of channels, we will be able to nurture interests—music, books, collecting, movies, golfing, carpentry, etc.—in a way that is utterly impossible with today's boob tube, where viewers are reduced to couch potatoes watching channels that can achieve profit-sized audiences only by appealing to the lowest common denominator.

What does all this have to do with obese, orchid-loving misogynist Nero Wolfe and milk-drinking, smart-alecky Archie Goodwin?

More than you might imagine. What better symbol of the power of the mind, of intellectual capital, than Nero Wolfe? Centuries ago his corpulence would have made his stay on earth a short one. He couldn't hunt or physically joust with his foes. Today, increasingly, mind matters more than matter. Wolfe's ability to fight crime with his intellect will be less "fictional" in the information age. And as technology empowers individuals, readers will better appreciate Wolfe's determination to make the universe revolve around him and his unalterable daily schedule instead of around the agendas of others. The time of top-down, military-style corporations, schools, and governments is coming to a close.

But Wolfe's continued appeal will be based on more than his intellect. He is cultivated. He has taste. He is educated. He has standards; perhaps not always "politically correct" but deeply felt. His misogyny may offend some, yet most women will appreciate his impeccable manners and his unwillingness to behave like a dirty old man. In short, Wolfe has character and integrity. And as these virtues enjoy a revival—which they will, thanks in no small part to a high technology that shatters the passivity-inducing, take-it-or-leave-it dominance of network TV—his popularity will grow. He stands as a rebuke to today's moral relativism.

Similarly, the Wolfe mysteries will enjoy renewed appreciation for their refusal to pander to baser instincts such as sex and violence. Rex Stout treats the reader as an intelligent being rather than a lustful lout longing for erotic stimulation or thirsting for blood. We will admire as never before the superdetective's disdain for vulgarity.

Wolfe, of course, has flaws. Humanizing qualities include his moods—he can go into a funk like the rest of us—and the need for money to maintain his extraordinary life-style. But while he may sometimes stoop to our level, he still manages to awe and inspire us. His girth comes not from potato chips and other junk foods but from a fine appreciation of what a superb chef can create. His obesity softens his snobbery. (And why some brewery hasn't tempted Wolfe to help give it an upscale image remains a mystery.) Despite his shortcomings, both his mind and, yes, his discipline enable him to perform superhuman deeds.

Archie Goodwin? He displays another side of intellectual capital—street smarts, or good common sense.

How would Nero Wolfe, in this age of the microchip, react to personal computers? One might think he would contemptuously dismiss these contraptions. But that would be underestimating our hero. He would rightly observe that they are still not very "user-friendly." Contrary to expectation, though, he would quickly grasp how useful their information prowess can be. Archie would make full use of them as well, although he wouldn't employ them with Wolfe's verve and imagination.

Too Many Clients highlights some of the special characteristics of a Rex Stout mystery:

Money. "There was nothing wrong with his long, bony face and broad forehead, but he simply didn't have the air of a man who might make a sizable contribution to Nero Wolfe's bank balance. . . . With no prospect of a fat fee in sight, it was beginning to look as if a trip to the safe deposit box might be called for before the Fourth of July."

Eye for telling detail. "Another point against him was that he had no hat. Ninety-eight percent of men who can pay big fees wear hats. . . . The tops of his sox, gray with little red dots, were down nearly to his shoes." (This book was written before John F. Kennedy went hatless to his inauguration. His topless example soon made hats old hat.)

Food. "When we are at table in the dining room for lunch or dinner, any attention of business is taboo. . . . Wolfe feels strongly that when a man is feeding, nothing should interfere with his concentration on his palate."

One can't imagine many writers today writing a book like *Too Many Clients*—about the murder of a high-powered, sex-crazed business executive—with Stout's nonprurient, critical detachment.

As the high-tech era unfolds, the stock of Stout, Wolfe, and Goodwin will reach new highs.

—Malcolm Forbes, Jr.

Too Many Clients

Chapter 1

When he had got deposited in the red leather chair I went to my desk, whirled my chair to face him, sat, and regarded him politely but without enthusiasm. It was only partly that his $39.95 suit didn't fit and needed pressing and his $3.00 shirt was on its second or third day; it was more him than his clothes. There was nothing wrong with his long bony face and broad forehead, but he simply didn't have the air of a man who might make a sizable contribution to Nero Wolfe's bank balance.

Which at that moment, that Monday afternoon in early May, was down to $14,194.62, after deducting the checks I had just drawn and put on Wolfe's desk for him to sign. That may look fairly respectable, but. What with the weekly wages of Theodore Horstmann, the orchid valet, Fritz Brenner, chef and house steward, and me, the handy man; and with grocery bills, including such items as the fresh caviar which Wolfe sometimes stirred into his coddled eggs at breakfast; and with the various needs of the orchids in the plant rooms up on the roof of the old brownstone, not to mention new additions to the collection; and with this and that and these and those, the minimum monthly outgo of that establishment averaged more than five grand. Also, the June 15 income-tax installment would be due in five weeks. So, with no prospect of a fat fee in sight, it was beginning to look as if a trip to the safe-deposit box might be called for before the Fourth of July.

Therefore, when the doorbell had rung and, going to the hall for a look through the one-way glass of the front door, I had seen an adult male stranger with no sample case, it had seemed fitting to open the door wide and give him a cordial eye. He had said, "This is Nero Wolfe's house, isn't it?" and I had said yes but Mr. Wolfe wouldn't be available until six o'clock, and he had said, "I know, he's up in the plant rooms from four to six, but I want to see Archie Goodwin. You're Mr. Goodwin?" I had admitted it and asked him what about, and he had said he wanted to consult me professionally. By then I had sized him up, or thought I had, and it didn't look very promising, but time could be wasted with him as well as without him, so I had taken him to the office. Another point against him was that he had no hat. Ninety-eight per cent of men who can pay big fees wear hats.

Leaning back in the red leather chair with his chin lowered and his intelligent gray eyes aimed at me, he spoke. "I'll have to tell you who I am, of course."

I shook my head. "Not unless it's material."

"It is." He crossed his legs. The tops of his socks, gray with little red dots, were down nearly to his shoes. "Else there was no use coming. I want to consult you in the strictest confidence."

I nodded. "Naturally. But this is Nero Wolfe's office, and I work for him. If you get a bill it will be from him."

"I know." Apparently that was a triviality. His eyes *were* intelligent. "I expect a bill and I'll pay it. I can speak in assured confidence?"

"Certainly. Unless you're loaded with something too heavy for me to hold, like murder or treason."

He smiled. "Other sins only speak; murder shrieks out. Treason doth never prosper. I am loaded with neither. None of my crimes is statutory. Then in confidence, Mr. Goodwin, my name is Yeager, Thomas G. Yeager. You may possibly have seen or heard it, though I am no celebrity. I live at Three-forty East Sixty-eighth Street. My firm, of which I am executive vice-president, is Continental Plastic Products, with offices in the Empire State Building."

I did not blink. Continental Plastic Products might be a giant with three or four floors, or it might have two small rooms with the only phone on the executive vice-president's desk. Even so, I knew that block of East 68th Street, and it was no slum, far from it. This character might wear a $39.95 suit because he didn't give a damn and didn't have to. I know a chairman of the board of a billion-dollar corporation, one of the 2 per cent, who never gets his shoes shined and shaves three times a week.

I had my notebook and was writing in it. Yeager was saying, "My phone number is not listed. It's Chisholm five, three-two-three-two. I came at a time when I knew Wolfe would be busy, to see you, because there's no point in explaining it to him since he would merely assign you to it. I think I am being followed, and I want to make sure, and if I am I want to know who is following me."

"That's kindergarten stuff." I tossed the notebook on my desk. "Any reputable agency will handle that for you at ten dollars an hour. Mr. Wolfe has a different approach to the fee question."

"I know he has. That's unimportant." He waved it away. "But it's vitally important to find out if I'm being followed, and quickly, and especially who it is. What agency at ten dollars an hour would have a man as good as you?"

"That's not the point. Even if I'm only half as good as I think I am it would still be a pity to waste me on spotting a tail. And what if there's no tail to spot? How long would it take to convince you? Say ten days, twelve hours a day, at a hundred dollars an hour. Twelve thousand bucks plus expenses. Even if you—"

"It wouldn't be ten days." He had lifted his chin. "I'm sure it wouldn't. And it wouldn't be twelve hours a day. If you'll let me explain, Mr. Goodwin. I think I am being followed only at certain times, or that I will be. Specifically, I suspect that I shall be followed when I leave my house this evening at seven o'clock to go crosstown, across the park, to an address on Eighty-second Street. One-fifty-six West Eighty-second Street. Perhaps the best plan would be for you to be at my house when I leave, but of course I shall leave the tactics to you. I don't want to be followed to that address. I don't want it known that I have any connection with it. If I am not followed, that would end it for today, and I would call on you again only when I intend to go there again."

"When would that be?"

"I can't say definitely. Possibly later in the week, perhaps some day next week. I could notify you a day in advance."

"How will you go, your car or a taxi?"

"Taxi."

"Which is more important to you, not to be followed to that address, or to know whether you're followed or not, or to identify the tail if you have one?"

"They're all important."

"Well." I screwed my lips. "I admit it's a little special. I mentioned a hundred dollars an hour, but that's for routine. The shoe would have to fit the foot, with Mr. Wolfe doing the fitting and you the footing."

He smiled. "There will be no difficulty about that. Then I'll expect you around seven. A little before?"

"Probably." I got my notebook. "Will the tail be someone you know?"

"I don't know. It might be."

"Man or woman?"

"I couldn't say. I don't know."

"An operative or a do-it-yourself?"

"I don't know. It could be either."

"Spotting him will be simple. Then what? If he's an operative I might recognize him, but that wouldn't help much. Of course I can pull him off whether I recognize him or not, but I can't squeeze his client's name out of him."

"But you can pull him off?"

"Sure. How much would the client's name be worth to you? It might come high."

"I don't think . . ." He hesitated. "I don't believe I would care to do that."

That didn't seem to fit, but I skipped it. "If it's someone on his own, of course I'll pull him off, and what else? Do you want him to know he's been spotted?"

He considered it for three seconds. "I think not. Better not, I think."

"Then I can't snap a picture of him. I can only give you a description."

"That will suffice."

"Okay." I dropped the notebook on my desk. "Your address on Sixty-eighth Street, that's not an apartment building, is it?"

"No, it's a house. My house."

"Then I shouldn't enter it and I shouldn't get too near it. If it's an operative he would probably recognize me. This is how it will be. At seven o'clock on the dot you will leave the house, walk to Second Avenue—don't cross it—and turn left. About thirty paces from the corner is a lunchroom, and in front—"

"How do you happen to know that?"

"There aren't many blocks in Manhattan I don't know. In front of the lunchroom, either at the curb or double-parked, a blue and yellow taxi will be standing with the driver in it and the flag down. The driver will have a big square face and big ears. You will say to him, 'You need a shave,' and he will say, 'My face is tender.' To make sure, when you get in look at his name on the card. It will be Albert Goller." I spelled it. "Do you want to write it down?"

"No."

"Then don't forget it. Give him the address on West Eighty-second Street and sit back and relax. That's all for you. Whatever the driver does, he'll know what he's doing. Don't keep looking back; that might make it a little harder."

He was smiling. "It didn't take you long to set the stage, did it?"

"I haven't got long." I glanced up at the clock on the wall. "It's nearly five." I stood up. "I'll be seeing you, but you won't be seeing me."

"Wonderful," he said, leaving the chair. "Measure your mind's height by the shade it casts. I knew you would be the man for it." He moved and offered a hand. "Don't bother to show me out, I know the way."

I went along, as always for some years, ever since the day a visitor left the door unlatched, sneaked back in, and hid behind the couch in the front room, and during the night went through everything in the office he could open. At the door I asked him what the name of the hackie would be, and he told me. Returning, I went on past the door of the office to the kitchen, got a glass from the shelf and a carton of milk from the refrigerator. Fritz, at the center table mincing shallots, gave me a look and spoke.

"That is an insult. I pull your nose. My shad roe *aux fines herbes* is a dish for a king."

"Yeah, but I'm not a king." I poured milk. "Also I'm leaving soon on an errand and I don't know when I'll be back."

"Ah? A personal errand."

"No." I took a sip. "I'll not only answer your question, I'll ask it for you. Having noticed that we haven't had a client worth a damn for nearly six weeks, you want to know if we have one now, and I don't blame you. It's possible but not likely. It looks like more peanuts." I took a sip. "You may have to invent a dish for a king made of peanut butter."

"Not impossible, Archie. The problem would be to crack the oil. Not vinegar; it would take too much. Perhaps lime juice, with or without a drop or two of onion juice. I'll try it tomorrow."

I told him to let me know how he made out, took the milk to the office, got at the phone at my desk, dialed the number of the *Gazette*, and got Lon Cohen. He said he was too busy to spare time for anything but a front-page lead or an invitation to a poker game. I said I was out of both items at the moment but would put them on back order, and meanwhile I would hold the line while he went to the morgue to see if they had anything on Thomas G. Yeager, executive vice-president of Continental Plastic Products, residing at 340 East 68th Street. He said he knew the name, they probably had a file on him, and he would send for it and call back. In ten minutes he did so. Continental Plastic Products was one of the big ones; its main plant was in Cleveland, and its sales and executive offices were in the Empire State Building. Thomas G. Yeager had been its executive vice-president for five years and was in the saddle. He was married and had a daughter, Anne, unmarried, and a son, Thomas G. Junior, married. He was a member of . . .

I told Lon that was all I needed, thanked him, hung up, and buzzed the plant rooms on the house phone. After a wait Wolfe's voice came, gruff of course.

"Yes?"

"Sorry to interrupt. A man named Yeager came. He wants to know if he is being tailed and by whom. He expects to be soaked and doesn't mind because no one but me is good enough. I have checked on him and he can stand it, and I might as well earn a couple of weeks' pay. I'll be gone when you come down. His name and address are in my notebook. I'll be back before bedtime."

"And tomorrow? How long will it last?"

"It won't. If it does we'll get Saul or Fred. I'll explain later. It's just a chore."

"Very well." He hung up, and I took the phone and dialed a number that would get me Al Goller.

Chapter 2

Two hours later, at twenty minutes past seven, I was sitting in a taxi parked on 67th Street between Second and Third Avenues, twisted around for a view through the rear window. If Yeager had left his house at 7:00 sharp, he should have been in Al Goller's cab by 7:04, and Al should have turned the corner onto 67th Street by 7:06. But it was 7:20, and no sign of him.

It was useless trying to guess what the hitch was, so I did. By 7:30 I had a collection of a dozen guesses, both plain and fancy. At 7:35 I was too annoyed to bother to guess. At 7:40 I told Mike Collins, the hackie, who was no stranger, "Nuts. I'll take a look," got out, and walked to the corner. Al was still there in his cab in front of the lunchroom. When the light showed green I crossed the avenue, went on to the cab, and asked Al, "Where is he?"

He yawned. "All I know is where he isn't."

"I'll ring him. If he comes while I'm inside, have trouble starting your engine until I come out and go. Give me time to get back to Mike."

He nodded and started another yawn, and I went into the lunchroom, found the phone booth in the rear, and dialed CH5-3232. After four rings I had a male voice in my ear. "Mrs. Yeager's residence."

"May I speak with Mr. Yeager?"

"He's not available at the moment. Who is this, please?"

I hung up. Not only did I know the voice of Sergeant Purley Stebbins of Homicide West, but also it was I who some years back had informed him that when one answers the phone at the home of the John Does one says not "Mr. Doe's residence" but "Mrs. Doe's residence." So I hung up, departed, signed to Al Goller to stay put, walked to the corner of 68th Street and turned right, and proceeded far enough to see that the dick behind the wheel of the PD car double-parked in front of Number 340 was the one who usually drove Stebbins. Whirling, I went back the way I had come, to the lunchroom and the phone booth, dialed the number of the *Gazette*, asked for Lon Cohen, and got him. My intention was to ask him if he had heard of any interesting murders recently, but I didn't get to.

His voice came. "Archie?"

"Right. Have you—"

"How the hell did you know Thomas G. Yeager was going to be murdered when you called me three hours ago?"

"I didn't. I don't. I merely—"

"Balls. But I appreciate it. Thanks for a page-one box. NERO WOLFE SCOOPS THE COPS AGAIN. I'm writing it now: 'Nero Wolfe, private eye extraordinary, was plunging into the Yeager murder case more than two hours before the body was discovered in an excavation on West Eighty-second

Street. At five-five P.M. his lackey, Archie Goodwin, phoned the *Gazette* office to get—'"

"You'll eat it. The whole world knows I'm not a lackey, I'm a flunky, and the idea of Nero Wolfe plunging. Besides, this is the first time I've phoned you for a month. If someone called and imitated my voice it was probably the murderer, and if you had been smart enough to keep him on while you had the call traced you might have—"

"Okay. Start over. When can you give me something?"

"When I have something to give. I always do, don't I? Pretend I didn't know Yeager had been murdered until you told me. Where is the excavation on West Eighty-second Street?"

"Between Columbus and Amsterdam."

"When was the body found?"

"Ten after seven. Fifty minutes ago. Under a tarp at the bottom of a hole dug by Con Edison. Boys climbed in to retrieve a ball that had rolled in."

I took a second. "The body must have rolled in since five o'clock; that's when Con Ed men usually quit if it's not an emergency. Didn't anyone see it roll in and pull the tarp over it?"

"How do I know? We got it only half an hour ago."

"How sure is the identification?"

"Positive. One of the men we sent knew him. He phoned just five minutes ago."

"How do you know he was murdered?"

"That's not official yet, but there's a hole in the side of his head that he didn't make with his finger. Look, Archie. His file from the morgue was here on my desk when the flash came. Within an hour everybody here will know that I sent for it two hours in advance. I don't mind being mysterious, but it could be a nuisance if this gets big. So I mention that I sent for the file because of a call from you, and someone who likes to do favors mentions it to someone at Homicide, and then?"

"Then I cooperate with the cops as usual. I'll be there in twenty minutes."

"Fine. It'll be a pleasure to see you."

I went out to the sidewalk, got into Al's cab, and told him to roll around the corner to Mike. As he pulled away from the curb he said his instructions were to accept only a passenger who told him he needed a shave, and I told him all right, he needed a shave. There was no space at the curb on 67th Street near Mike, so we stopped alongside, and I got out and stood between the two cabs, at the open front windows.

"The party's off," I told them. "Circumstances beyond my control. I mentioned no figure to you because of unknown factors, such as how long it would take, but since you have only had to sit around a while, maybe twenty apiece would be enough. What do you think?"

Mike said, "Yeah," and Al said, "Sure. What happened?"

I got out my wallet and took out six twenties. "So we'll make it three times that," I said, "because you are not dumb. I haven't told you the name of the client, but I described him, and you know he was coming from around the corner on Sixty-eighth Street, and he was going to West Eighty-second Street. So when you read in the paper tomorrow about a man named Thomas G. Yeager who lived at Three-forty East Sixty-eighth Street, that his body was found at seven-ten this evening in a hole on West Eighty-second Street, with a hole in his head, you will wonder. When a man wonders about something, he likes to talk about it. So here's sixty bucks apiece. What I want is a chance to satisfy my curiosity without being bothered by cops wanting to know why I arranged this setup. Why the hell did he go on his own instead of sticking to our program? I will add that he didn't say or hint that he expected or feared any violence; he only wanted to find out if he was being tailed, and if so he wanted the tail pulled off and identified if possible. That's what I told you and that's how it was. I haven't the faintest idea who killed him or why. You know all I know. I would just as soon have nobody else know it until I look around a little. You guys have known me— how long?"

"Five years," Mike said.

"Eight years," Al said. "How did you find out he got it? If his body was found only an hour ago—"

"When I rang his house I recognized the voice that answered, a Homicide sergeant, Purley Stebbins. When I went around the corner I recognized the driver of a PD car parked in front of Number Three-forty. When I phoned a newspaperman I know and asked for news I got it. I am saving nothing; you have it all. Here's your sixty bucks."

Al reached to get a corner of one twenty with a finger and a thumb and slipped it out. "This'll do," he said. "This is enough for my time, and keeping my lip buttoned is just personal. I'll enjoy it. Every cop I see I can think, You bastard, what I know and you don't."

Mike, grinning, took his three twenties. "I'm different," he said. "Just as apt as not I'd tell everybody in reach, including cops, but now I can't because I'd have to give your forty bucks back. I may not be noble but I'm honest." He put the bills in a pocket and extended a paw. "But we'd better shake on it just to be sure."

We shook, and I got back into Al's cab and told him to take me to the *Gazette* building.

If Lon Cohen had a title, I didn't know what it was and I doubt if he did. Just his name was on the door of the little room on the twentieth floor, two doors down from the corner office of the publisher, and in that situation you would think he would be out of the dust stirred up by the daily whirlwind of a newspaper, but he always seemed to be up, not only on what had just happened but on what was just going to happen. We kept no account of how we stood on give and take over the years, but it pretty well evened up.

He was very dark—dark skin stretched tight over his neat little face, dark brown deep-set eyes, hair almost black, slicked back and up over his sloping dome. He was next to the best of the poker players I occasionally spent a night with, the best being Saul Panzer, whom you will meet later. When I entered the little room that Monday evening he was on the phone, and I took the chair at the end of his desk and sat and listened. It went on for minutes, and all he said was "No" nine times. When he hung up I said, "Just a yes man."

"I have to make a call," he said. "Here, pass the time." He picked up a cardboard folder and handed it to me and returned to the phone.

It was the file on Thomas G. Yeager. Not bulky—a dozen or so newspaper clippings, four typewritten memos, tear sheets of an article in a trade journal, *Plastics Today*, and three photo-graphs. Two of the photographs were studio jobs with his name typed at the bottom, and one was of a gathering in the Churchill ballroom, with a typed caption pasted on: "Thomas G. Yeager speaking at the banquet of the National Plastics Association, Churchill Hotel, New York City, October 19, 1958." He was at the mike on the stage with his arm raised for a gesture. I read the memos and glanced through the clippings, and was looking over the article when Lon finished at the phone and turned.

"All right, give," he demanded.

I closed the folder and put it on the desk. "I came," I said, "to make a deal, but first you should know something. I have never seen Thomas G. Yeager or spoken with him or had any communica-tion from him, and neither has Mr. Wolfe. I know absolutely nothing about him except what you told me on the phone and what I just read in that folder."

Lon was smiling. "Okay for the record. Now just between you and me."

"The same, believe it or not. But I heard some-thing just before I phoned you at five o'clock that made me curious about him. For the time being I would prefer to keep what I heard to myself—for at least twenty-four hours and maybe longer. I expect to be busy and I don't want to spend tomorrow at the DA's office. So it's not necessary for anyone to know that I rang you this afternoon to ask about Yeager."

"It may be desirable. For me. I sent for his file. If I say I dreamed something was going to happen to him people might talk."

I grinned at him. "Come off it. You haven't even

got a pair. You can say anything you damn please. You can say someone told you something off the record and you're hanging on to it. Besides, I'm offering a deal. If you'll forget about my curiosity about Yeager until further notice, I'll put you on my Christmas card list. This year it will be an abstract painting in twenty colors and the message will be 'We want to share with you this picture of us bathing the dog, greetings of the season from Archie and Mehitabel and the children.'"

"You haven't got a Mehitabel or any children."

"Sure, that's why it will be abstract."

He eyed me. "You could give me something not for quotation. Or something to hold until you're ready to let go."

"No. Not now. If and when, I know your number."

"As usual." He raised his hands, palms up. "I have things to do. Drop in some day." His phone rang, and he turned to it, and I went.

On my way to the elevator and going down, I looked it over. I had told Wolfe I would be back before bedtime, but it was only nine o'clock. I was hungry. I could go to a soda counter for a bite and decide how to proceed while I bit, but the trouble was that I knew darned well what I wanted to do, and it might take all night. Besides, although it was understood that when I was out on an errand I would be guided by intelligence and experience, as Wolfe had put it, it was also understood that if things got complicated I would phone. And the phone was no good for this, not only because he hated talking on the phone about anything whatever, but also because it had to be handled just right or he would refuse to play. So I flagged a taxi and gave the driver the address of the old brownstone on West 35th Street.

Arriving, I mounted the seven steps to the stoop and pushed the bell button. My key isn't enough when the chain bolt is on, as it usually is when I'm out. When Fritz opened the door and I entered, he tried not to look a question at me but couldn't keep it out of his eyes—the same question he hadn't asked that afternoon: Did we have a client? I told him it was still possible, and I was empty, and could he spare a hunk of bread and a glass of milk? He said but of course, he would bring it, and I went to the office.

Wolfe was at his desk with a book, leaning back in the only chair in the world that he can sit down in without making a face, made to order by his design and under his supervision. The reading light in the wall above and behind his left shoulder was the only one on in the room, and like that, with the light at that angle, he looks even bigger than he is. Like a mountain with the sun rising behind it. As I entered and flipped the wall switch to cut him down to size, he spoke. He said, "Umph." As I crossed to my desk he asked, "Have you eaten?"

"No." I sat. "Fritz is bringing something."

"Bringing?"

Surprise with a touch of annoyance. Ordinarily, when an errand has made me miss a meal and I come home hungry, I go to the kitchen to eat. The exceptions are when I have something to report that shouldn't wait, and when he is settled down for the evening with a book he is in no mood to listen to a report, no matter what.

I nodded. "I have something on my chest."

His lips tightened. The book, a big thick one,

was spread open, held with both hands. He closed it on a finger to keep his place, heaved a sigh, and demanded, "What?"

I decided it was useless to try circling around. With him you have to fit the tactics to the atmosphere. "That slip I put on your desk," I said. "The bank balance after drawing those checks. The June tax payment will be due in thirty-seven days. Of course we could file an amended declaration if someone doesn't turn up with a major problem and a retainer to match."

He was scowling at me. "Must you harp on the obvious?"

"I'm not harping. I haven't mentioned it for three days. I refer to it now because I would like to have permission to take a stab at digging up a client instead of sitting here on my fanny waiting for one to turn up. I'm getting calluses on my rump."

"And your modus? A sandwich board?"

"No, sir. I have a possible target, just barely possible. About that man who came to hire me to spot a tail, Thomas G. Yeager. I got two cabs and had them waiting at seven o'clock, one for him to take and one for me to follow in. He didn't show up. I got tired waiting and rang his house, and Purley Stebbins answered the phone. I went around a corner and there was a car with Purley's driver in it, in front of Yeager's house. I rang Lon Cohen and he wanted to know why I had phoned him to ask about Thomas G. Yeager two hours before Yeager's body was found in a hole on West Eighty-second Street. With a hole in his head. So our client was gone, but it occurred to me that his going might possibly get us another one. He was a big shot in his field, with a big title and a nice house in a nice neighborhood, and it could be that no one but me knew of his suspicion that he was being tailed or was going to be. Also the address that he thought he was going to be tailed to was One-fifty-six West Eighty-second Street, and it was in that block on that street that his body had been found. So I spent some of your money. Besides paying the two hackies for their time, I gave them an extra forty bucks to forget where they had been—that is, I gave it to Mike Collins. Al Goller preferred to do his forgetting for personal reasons."

Wolfe grunted. "*Your* initiative. They may already have the murderer."

"Then you're out forty dollars in addition to the fifty-three dollars and sixty cents spent on behalf of a client from whom we won't collect because he's dead. But it's not as simple as that. Actually our client is not dead. Or, putting it another way, we didn't have a client. On my way home I stopped in at the *Gazette* to ask Lon Cohen to forget that I had phoned to ask him about Thomas G. Yeager, and there was a folder on his desk with some items about Yeager, including three pictures of him, which I looked at. The man who came this afternoon to hire me to spot his tail was not Yeager. No resemblance. So I suppose it's more accurate to say we didn't have a client."

Chapter 3

Naturally I expected to get a strong reaction, and I did. Wolfe straightened up to reach to the desk for his bookmark, a thin strip of gold which he used only for books he considered worthy of a place on the shelves in the office. As he inserted it in the book Fritz appeared with a tray and brought it to my desk. Seeing that Wolfe was putting his book down, he winked at me approvingly, and I swiveled to get at the tray. There was a bowl of chestnut soup, a cucumber-and-shrimp sandwich on toast, a roast-beef sandwich on a hard roll, home-baked, a pile of watercress, an apple baked in white wine, and a glass of milk.

A question of etiquette. When we are at table in the dining room for lunch or dinner, any mention of business is taboo. The rule has never been formally extended to fill-ins, but Wolfe feels strongly that when a man is feeding nothing should interfere with his concentration on his palate. Having disposed of the book, he leaned back and shut his eyes. After a few spoonfuls of soup I said, "I'm too hungry to taste anyway. Go right ahead."

His eyes opened. "Beyond all doubt?"

"Yes, sir." I took in a spoonful and swallowed. "His name was typed on the pictures. Also there was a picture of him in a magazine. A face like a squirrel with a pointed nose and not much chin. The man this afternoon had a long bony face and broad forehead."

"And, calling himself Yeager, he said that he expected to be followed to a specified address on West Eighty-second Street, and Yeager's body was found near that address. How long had he been dead?"

"I don't know. Give them time. Besides what I've told you, all Lon knew was that the body was in a hole in the street dug by Con Edison men, it was covered with a tarp, and it was found by boys whose ball rolled in."

"If I approve of your proposal to explore the possibility of getting a client and earning a fee, how do you intend to proceed?"

I swallowed soup. "First I finish these sandwiches and the apple and milk. Then I go to Eighty-second Street. Since the body was found in a hole in the street, it's quite possible that there is nothing to connect it with that neighborhood or that particular address. He could have been killed anywhere and taken there and dumped. The blocks in the Eighties between Columbus and Amsterdam are no place for a big shot in a big corporation. The Puerto Ricans and Cubans average three or four to a room. I want to find out what business Yeager had there, if any."

"You would go now? Tonight?"

"Sure. As soon as I empty this tray."

"Pfui. How often have I told you that impetuosity is a virtue only when delay is dangerous?"

"Oh, six thousand."

"But you are still headlong. In the morning we shall get many details that are lacking now. There may be no problem left, except the identity of the man who came here in masquerade, and that may no longer be of interest. Now, of course, it is. How long was he with you?"

"Twenty-five minutes."

"We may need a record of what he said. Instead of dashing up to Eighty-second Street you will spend the evening at the typewriter. The conversation verbatim, and include a complete description." He picked up the book and shifted to his reading position.

That took care of the rest of the evening. I still would have liked to take a look at 156 West 82nd Street before the cops got interested in it, if they hadn't already, but Wolfe did have a point, and it was his money I had given Mike Collins. Typing my talk with the bogus Yeager was no strain, merely work. I have reported orally many conversations much longer than that one, with more people involved. It was a little short of midnight when I finished. After collating the sheets, original and carbon, and putting them in a drawer, removing the orchids from the vase on Wolfe's desk and taking them to the garbage pail in the kitchen—he wants them gone when he brings fresh ones in the morning—locking the safe, seeing that the front door was bolted, and turning out the lights, I mounted two flights to my room. Wolfe was already in his, on the second floor.

Usually I get down to the kitchen for breakfast around eight-thirty, but that Tuesday morning I made it earlier, a little after eight. I wanted to go straight to the little table where Fritz had put my copy of the *Times* on the reading rack, but impetuosity is a virtue only when delay is dangerous, so I made myself exchange greetings with Fritz, get my glass of orange juice, stir it, and take a couple of sips. Then I went and got the paper. Would the headline be YEAGER MURDER SOLVED?

It wasn't. It was EXECUTIVE SHOT AND KILLED. I sat down and took another sip.

With my orange juice, buckwheat cakes and sausage, blackberry jam, and two cups of coffee, I read it in both the *Times* and the *Gazette*. I'll skip such details as the names of the boys who found the body. They got their names in the papers, and that ought to last them, and anyway I doubt if they read books. He had been shot once, above the right ear, at close range, and had died instantly. He had been dead sixteen to twenty-four hours when the body was examined at 7:30 p.m., so he had been killed between 7:30 p.m. Sunday and 3:30 a.m. Monday. The autopsy might make it more definite. There had been no workmen in the excavation on 82nd Street all day Monday because needed repair times were not at hand, so the body could have been put in the hole Sunday night. The tarpaulin had been left in the hole by the workmen. No one had been found who had seen Yeager alive in the neighborhood or who had heard a shot fired in the vicinity, so he had probably been killed elsewhere and the body transferred there.

Yeager's daughter, Anne, was at college, Bennington. His son, Thomas G. Junior, was in Cleveland, employed at the plant of Continental Plastic Products. Yeager and his wife had left New York Friday evening to spend the weekend visiting

friends in the country; he had returned to town
Sunday afternoon, but his wife hadn't returned
until Monday morning. There had been no one at
the Yeager house on 68th Street Sunday afternoon.
Nothing was known of Yeager's movements after
he boarded a train for New York at Stamford at 5:02
p.m. Sunday.

No one was being held by the police, and the
District Attorney would say only that the investigation was in progress.

In the picture of him in the *Times* he was
grinning like a politician. There were two in the
Gazette—one a reproduction of one I had seen in
Lon's office, and one of him stretched out at the
edge of the hole he had been found in. I clipped
the one in the *Times* and the live one from the
Gazette and put them in my pocket notebook.

At 8:51 I put down my empty coffee cup,
thanked Fritz for the meal and told him I might or
might not be home for lunch, went to the hall,
mounted the flight to Wolfe's room, and entered.
His breakfast tray, with nothing left on it but empty
dishes, was on the table by a window, and beside it
was his copy of the *Times*. He was standing before
the mirror on the dresser, knotting his four-in-hand.
Since he always goes from his room to the roof for
his morning two hours in the plant rooms I don't
know why he sports a tie—maybe being polite to
the orchids. He grunted good morning, got the tie
adjusted, and turned.

"I'm off," I said. "Instructions?"

"*Your* initiative," he said.

"No, sir. That was yesterday. Are you sending
me or aren't you? Apparently it's wide open, unless
they're saving something. He had been dead at

least fourteen hours when that bozo came yesterday. What he said is in my desk drawer. How much do I have along for possible needs?"

"Enough."

"Any limit?"

"Certainly. The limit dictated by your discretion and sagacity."

"Right. Expect me when you see me."

Descending to the office, I opened the safe, got five hundred dollars in used fives, tens, and twenties from the cash reserve, closed the safe, and twirled the knob. Removing my jacket, I unlocked the bottom drawer of my desk, got my armpit holster and put it on, loaded the Marley .32, and slipped it in the holster. Ever since an unpleasant experience some years ago I never go on an errand connected with a murder with only my pocketknife. I put on my jacket and went to the hall. Coat and hat? I hate to bother with them. There was no sun outside; the 7:30 radio had said possible showers. What the hell, live dangerously. I left, walked to Tenth Avenue and flagged a taxi, and told the driver 82nd and Broadway.

Of course I had no script; it would have to be ad lib, except the obvious first step, to find out if the city scientists had finished their research. Many of them knew me by sight, and they knew I wouldn't be nosing around the scene of a murder just to pass the time. So, walking east from Broadway and crossing Amsterdam Avenue, I stopped at the corner for a survey from a distance, from the uptown side of 82nd Street. I have good eyes at any distance, and I could make out the "156" on a house about thirty paces from the corner. Parked cars were bumper to bumper along the curb on both sides except where barriers guarded the hole in the pavement, but there was no police car, marked or unmarked.

Begging the pardon of the tenants of the block, it was a slum. Fifty or sixty years ago, when the stone was new and clean and the brass was shiny, the long row of five-story houses might have been a credit to the city, but no more. They looked ratty and they were ratty, and it was a bet that they would crumble any minute if they hadn't been jammed together. There weren't many people on the sidewalk, and no kids, since it was school hours, but there was quite a gathering around the barriers surrounding the hole, which was some fifteen yards beyond Number 156. There was a cop there riding herd on them, but he was merely a flatfoot. There was no sign of Homicide or DA man.

I crossed the street and walked along to the barriers. Over the shoulder of a woman in a purple dress I could see two workmen down in the hole, so the scientists had finished with it. While I stood looking down at them my sagacity came up with five conclusions:

1. Yeager had had some connection with someone or something at Number 156. Whoever the guy was who had come and hired me, and whatever his game was, and whether he had killed Yeager or not, he certainly hadn't just pulled that address out of a hat.

2. If Yeager had been killed elsewhere and the body had been brought to this spot deliberately, to impress someone at 156, why hadn't it been dumped on the sidewalk smack in front of 156? Why roll it into the hole and climb down and put a tarp over it? No.

3. If Yeager had been killed elsewhere and the body had been brought to this spot not deliberately, but accidentally, merely because there was a hole here, you would have to swallow a coincidence that even a whale couldn't get down. No.

4. Yeager had not been shot as he was entering or leaving 156. At any time of night the sound of a shot in that street would have brought a dozen, a hundred, heads sticking out of windows. So the shooter runs or steps on the gas pedal. He does not drag the body to the hole and roll it in and climb down and put a tarp over it. No.

5. Therefore Yeager had been killed inside Number 156, some time, any time, after 7:30 p.m. Sunday, and later that night, when there was no audience, the body had been carried to the hole, only fifteen yards, and dropped in. That didn't account for the tarp, but no theory would. At least the tarp didn't hurt it. It could have been to postpone discovery of the body until the workmen came.

In detective work it's a great convenience to have a sagacity that can come up with conclusions like that; it saves wear and tear on the brain. I backed away from the barrier and walked the fifteen yards to Number 156.

Some of the houses had a sign, VACANCY, displayed at the entrance, but 156 didn't. But it did have a sign, hand-printed on a piece of cardboard fastened to the pillar at the foot of the steps going up to the stoop. It said SUPERENTENDANT, with an arrow pointing to the right. So I went right and down three steps, then left and through an open doorway into a little vestibule, and there in front of my eyes was evidence that there was something special about that house. The door had a Rabson lock. You have a Rabson installed on a door only if you insist on being absolutely certain that anyone who enters must have either the right key or a sledgehammer, and you are able and willing to shell out $61.50.

I pushed the bell button. In a moment the door opened, and there facing me was one of the three most beautiful females I have ever seen.

I must have gaped or gasped, from the way she smiled, the smile of a queen at a commoner. She spoke. "You want something?" Her voice was low and soft, without breath.

The only thing to say was "Certainly, I want you," but I managed to hold it in. She was eighteen, tall and straight, with skin the color of the wild thyme honey that Wolfe gets from Greece, and she was extremely proud of something, not her looks. When a woman is proud of her looks it's just a smirk. I don't think I stammered, but if I didn't I should have. "I'd like to see the superintendent."

"Are you a policeman?"

If she liked policemen the only thing to say was "Yes." But probably she didn't. "No," I said, "I'm a newspaperman."

"That's nice." She turned and called, "Father, a newspaperman!" and her voice raised was even more wonderful than her voice low. She turned back to me, graceful as a big cat, and stood there straight and proud, not quite smiling, her warm dark eyes as curious as if she had never seen a man before. I knew damn well I ought to say something, but what? The only thing to say was "Will you marry me?" but that wouldn't do because the idea of her washing dishes or darning socks was preposterous.

Then I became aware of something, that I had moved my foot inside the sill so the door couldn't close, and that spoiled it. I was just a private detective trying to dig up a client.

Footsteps sounded, and as they approached she moved aside. It was a man, a chunky broad-shouldered guy two inches shorter than her, with a pug nose and bushy eyebrows. I stepped inside and greeted him. "My name's Goodwin. From the *Gazette*. I want to rent a room, a front room."

He said to his daughter, "Go, Maria," and she turned and went, down the dark hall. He turned to me. "No rooms."

"A hundred dollars a week," I said. "I'm going to do an article on the scene of a murder after the murder. I want to take pictures of the people who come to look at it. A window on your second floor would be just the right angle."

"I said no rooms." His voice was deep and rough.

"You can shift someone around. Two hundred dollars."

"No."

"Three hundred."

"No."

"Five hundred."

"You're crazy. No."

"I'm not crazy. You are. Snooting five hundred bucks. What's your name?"

"It's *my* name."

"Oh for God's sake. I can get it next door or from the cop out front. What's wrong with it?"

He half closed one eye. "Nothing is wrong with it. My name is Cesar Perez. I am a citizen of the United States of America."

"So am I. Will you rent me a room for one week for five hundred dollars in advance in cash?"

"But what I said." He gestured with both hands and both shoulders. "No room. That man out there dead, this is a bad thing. To take pictures of the people from this house, no. Even if there was a room."

I decided to be impetuous. Delay could actually be dangerous, since Homicide or the DA might uncover a connection between Yeager and this house any moment. Getting my case from my pocket and taking an item from it, I handed it to him. "Can you see in this light?" I asked.

He didn't try. "What is it?"

"My license. I'm not a newspaperman, I'm a private detective, and I'm investigating the murder of Thomas G. Yeager."

He half closed an eye again. He poked the license at me, and I took it. His chest swelled with an intake of air. "You're not a policeman?"

"No."

"Then get out of here. Get out of this house. I have told three different policemen I don't know anything about that man in the hole, and one of them insulted me. You get out."

"All right," I said, "it's your house." I returned the license to the case and the case to my pocket. "But I'll tell you what will happen if you bounce me. Within half an hour a dozen policemen will take the house over, with a search warrant. They'll go over every inch of it. They'll round up everybody here, beginning with you and your daughter, and they'll nab everyone who enters. The reason they'll do that is that I'll tell them I can prove that Thomas G.

Yeager came to this house Sunday evening and he was killed here."

"That's a lie. Like that policeman. That's insult."

"Okay. First I call to the cop out front to come in and stand by so you can't warn anyone." I turned. I had hit it. With the cops of course he had been set, but I had been unexpected and had caught him off balance. And he wasn't a moron. He knew that even if I couldn't prove it I must have enough to sick the law on him and the house.

As I turned he reached and got my sleeve. I turned back, and he stood there, his jaw working. I asked, not hostile, just wanting to know, "Did you kill him?"

"You're a policeman," he said.

"I am not. My name is Archie Goodwin and I work for a private detective named Nero Wolfe. We expect to get paid for investigating this case, that's how we make a living. So I'll be honest; we would rather find out for ourselves why Yeager came here instead of having the police do it, but if you won't cooperate I'll have to call that cop in. Did you kill him?"

He wheeled and started down the hall. I moved, got his shoulder, and yanked him around. "Did you kill him?"

"I've got a knife," he said. "In this house I've got a right to have it."

"Sure. I've got this." I pulled the Marley from the holster. "And a permit for it. Did you kill him?"

"No. I want to see my wife. She thinks better than I do. My wife and daughter. I want—"

A door ten feet down the hall swung open, and a woman's voice said, "We're here, Cesar," and there they were. The one coming was a tall grim-faced woman with an air of command. Maria stayed at the door. Perez started reeling off Spanish at his wife, but she broke in.

"Stop it! He'll think it's secrets. With an American talk American." She focused sharp black eyes on me. "We heard you. I knew this would come, only I thought it would be the police. My husband is an honest man. He did not kill Mr. Yeager. We call him Mr. House because it's his house. How do you know?"

I returned the Marley to the holster. "Since I do know, Mrs. Perez, does it matter how?"

"No, I am a fool to ask. All right, ask questions."

"I'd rather have your husband answer them. It may take a while. If there's a room with chairs?"

"I'll answer them. We sit down with friends. You after my husband with a gun."

"I was only showing off. Okay, if your legs can stand it mine can. What time did Mr. Yeager come here Sunday?"

"I thought you knew."

"I do. I'm finding out how you answer questions. If you answer too many of them wrong I'll try your husband, or the police will."

She considered it a moment. "He came around seven o'clock."

"Did he come to see you or your husband or your daughter?"

She glared. "No."

"Whom did he come to see?"

"I don't know. We don't know."

"Try again. That's silly. I'm not going to spend all day prying it out of you bit by bit."

She eyed me. "Have you ever been up there?"

"I'm asking the questions, Mrs. Perez. Whom did he come to see?"

"We don't know." She turned. "Go, Maria."

"But Mother, it's not—"

"Go!"

Maria went, back inside, and shut the door. It was just as well, since it's a strain to keep your eyes where they ought to be when they want to be somewhere else. Mother returned to me.

"He came around seven o'clock and knocked on the door. That one." She pointed to the door Maria had shut behind her. "He spoke to my husband and paid him some money. Then he went down the hall to the elevator. We don't know if someone was up there or if someone came later. We were looking at the television, so we wouldn't hear if someone came in and went to the elevator. Anyhow we weren't supposed to know. The door in front has a good lock. So it's not silly that we don't know who he came to see."

"Where's the elevator?"

"In the back. It has a lock too."

"You asked if I have ever been up there. Have you?"

"Of course. Every day. We keep it clean."

"Then you have a key. We'll go up now." I moved.

She glanced at her husband, hesitated, glanced at me, went and opened the door Maria had closed and said something in Spanish, and started down the hall. Perez followed, and I brought up the rear. At the far end of the hall, clear back, she took a key from a pocket of her skirt and inserted it in the lock of a metal door, another Rabson lock. The door, either aluminum or stainless steel, slid open. That

door certainly didn't fit that hall, and neither did
the inside of the elevator—more stainless steel,
with red enameled panels on three sides. It was
small, not even as large as Wolfe's at home. It
ascended, silent and smooth, I judged, right to the
top floor, the door slid open, and we stepped out.

For the second time in an hour I must have either
gaped or gasped when Perez turned on the lights. I
have seen quite a few rooms where people had gone
all out, but that topped them all. It may have been
partly the contrast with the neighborhood, the outside of the house, and the down below, but it would
have been remarkable no matter where. The first
impression was of silk and skin. The silk, mostly red
but some pale yellow, was on the walls and ceiling and
couches. The skin was on the girls and women in the
pictures, paintings, that took a good third of the wall
space. In all directions was naked skin. The pale
yellow carpet, wall to wall, was silk too, or looked it.
The room was enormous, twenty-five feet wide and
the full length of the house, with no windows at either
end. Headed to the right wall, near the center, was a
bed eight feet square with a pale yellow silk coverlet.
Since yellow was Wolfe's pet color it was too bad he
hadn't come along. I sniffed the air. It was fresh
enough, but it smelled. Air-conditioned, with built-in
perfume.

There weren't many surfaces that would hold
fingerprints—the tops of two tables, a TV console,
a stand with a telephone. I turned to Mrs. Perez.
"Have you cleaned here since Sunday night?"

"Yes, yesterday morning."

That settled that. "Where's the door to the stairs?"

"No stairs."

"They're boarded up below," Perez said.

"The elevator's the only way to come up?"

"Yes."

"How long has it been like this?"

"Four years. Since he bought the house. We had been here two years."

"How often did he come here?"

"We don't know."

"Certainly you do, if you came up every day to clean. How often?"

"Maybe once a week, maybe more."

I turned on Perez. "Why did you kill him?"

"No." He half closed an eye. "Me? No."

"Who did?"

"We don't know," his wife said.

I ignored her. "Look," I told him. "I don't want to turn you over unless I have to. Mr. Wolfe and I would prefer to keep you to ourselves. But if you don't open up we'll have no choice, and there may not be much time. They've got a lot of fingerprints from the tarpaulin that covered his body. I know he was killed in this house. If just one of those prints matches yours, good-by. You're in. Since he was killed in this house, you know *something*. What?"

He said to his wife, "Felita?"

She was looking at me, her sharp black eyes into me. "You're a private detective," she said. "You told my husband that's how you make a living. So we pay you. We have some money, not much. One hundred dollars."

"What do you pay me for?"

"To be our detective."

"And detect what?"

"We'll tell you. We have the money downstairs."

"I'll earn it first. All right, I'm your detective, but I can quit any time, for instance if I decide that you or your husband killed Yeager. What do you want me to detect?"

"We want you to help us. What you said about the fingerprints. I told him he must put on gloves, but he didn't. We don't know how you know so much, but we know how it will be if you tell the police about this house. We did not kill Mr. House. Mr. Yeager. We don't know who killed him. My husband took his dead body and put it in that hole because we had to. When he came Sunday evening he told my husband to go to Mondor's at midnight and bring some things he had ordered, some caviar and roast pheasant and other things, and when my husband came up with them his dead body was here." She pointed. "There on the floor. What could we do? It was secret that he came to this house. What would happen if we called a policeman? We knew what would happen. So now we pay you to help us. Perhaps more than one hundred dollars. You will know—"

She whirled around. There had been a noise from the elevator, a click, and then a faint sound of friction, barely audible. Perez said, "It's going down. Someone down there."

"Yeah," I agreed. "Who?"

"We don't know," Mrs. Perez said.

"Then we'll see. Stay where you are, both of you." I got the Marley out.

"It's a policeman," Perez said.

"No," she said. "No key. He couldn't have Mr. House's keys because we took them."

"Shut up," I told them. "If I'm your detective, do what I say. No talking and no moving."

We stood facing the elevator. I moved to the wall and put my back to it, arm's length from the elevator door. Since it had been up when the visitor came and he had had to push the button to bring it down, he must know someone was up here and might come out with his finger on a trigger, which was where I had mine. The faint sound came again, then a click, the door opened, and out came a woman. Her back was to me as she faced Mrs. Perez.

"Thank God," she said, "it's you. I thought it would be."

"We don't know you," Mrs. Perez said.

I did. I had taken a step and got her profile. It was Meg Duncan, whom I had seen last week from a fifth-row seat on the aisle, in her star part in *The Back Door to Heaven*.

Chapter 4

If you ever have your pick of being jumped by a man your size or a woman who only comes to your chin, I advise you to make it the man. If he's unarmed the chances are that the very worst he'll do is floor you, but God knows what the woman will do. And you may floor him first, but you can't plug a woman. Meg Duncan came at me exactly the way a cavewoman went at her man, or some other man, ten thousand years ago, her claws reaching for me and her mouth open ready to bite. There were only two alternatives, to get too far or too close, and too close is better. I rammed into her past the claws, against her, and wrapped her, and in one second the breath was all out of her. Her mouth stayed open, but for air, not to bite. I slid around and had her arms from behind. In that position the worst you can get is a kick on a shin. She was gasping. My grip may have been really hurting her right arm because I had the gun in that hand and the butt was pressing into her. When I removed that hand to drop the Marley in my pocket she didn't move, and I turned loose and backed up a step.

"I know who you are," I said. "I caught your

show last week and you were wonderful. I'm not a cop, I'm a private detective. I work for Nero Wolfe. When you get your breath you'll tell me why you're here."

She turned, slowly. It took her five seconds to make the half-turn to face me. "You hurt me," she said.

"No apology. A squeeze and a little bruise on an arm are nothing to what you had in mind."

She rubbed the arm, her head tilted back to look up at me, still breathing through her mouth. I was being surprised that I had recognized her. On the stage she was extremely easy on the eyes. Now she was just a thirty-year-old female with a good enough face, in a plain gray suit and a plain little hat, but of course she was under strain.

She spoke. "Are you Nero Wolfe's Archie Goodwin?"

"No. I'm my Archie Goodwin. I'm Nero Wolfe's confidential assistant."

"I know about you." She was getting enough air through her nose. "I know you're a gentleman." She extended a hand to touch my sleeve. "I came here to get something that belongs to me. I'll get it and go. All right?"

"What is it?"

"A—a something with my initials on it. A cigarette case."

"How did it get here?"

She tried to smile, as a lady to a gentleman, but it was a feeble effort. A famous actress should have done better, even under strain. "Does that matter, Mr. Goodwin? It's mine. I can describe it. It's dull gold, with an emerald in a corner on one side and my initials on the other."

I smiled as a gentleman to a lady. "When did you leave it here?"

"I didn't say I left it here."

"Was it Sunday evening?"

"No. I wasn't here Sunday evening."

"Did you kill Yeager?"

She slapped me. That is, she slapped at me. She was certainly impetuous. Also she was quick, but so was I. I caught her wrist and gave it a little twist, not enough to hurt much, and let go. There was a gleam in her eyes, and she looked more like Meg Duncan. "You're a man, aren't you?" she said.

"I can be. Right now I'm just a working detective. Did you kill Yeager?"

"No. Of course not." Her hand came up again, but only to touch my sleeve. "Let me get my cigarette case and go."

I shook my head. "You'll have to manage without it for a while. Do you know who killed Yeager?"

"Of course not." Her fingers curved around my arm, not a grip, just a touch. "I know I can't bribe you, Mr. Goodwin, I know enough about you to know that, but detectives do things for people, don't they? I can pay you to do something for me, can't I? If you won't let me get my cigarette case you can get it for me, and keep it for me. You can give it to me later, you can decide when, I don't care as long as you keep it." Her fingers pressed a little. "I would pay whatever you say. A thousand dollars?"

Things were looking up, but it was getting a little complicated. At 4:30 yesterday afternoon we had had no client and no prospect of any. Then one had come but had turned out to be a phony. Then Mrs. Perez had dangled a hundred bucks and perhaps more. Now this customer was offering a grand. I was digging up clients all right, but too many clients can be worse than too few.

I regarded her. "It might work," I said. "It's like this. Actually I can't take a job; I'm employed by Nero Wolfe. He takes the jobs. I'm going to look this place over, and if I find your cigarette case, as I will if it's here, I'll take it. Give me your keys, to the door down below and the elevator."

Her fingers left my arm. "Give them to you?"

"Right. You won't need them any more." I glanced at my wrist. "It's ten-thirty-five. You have no matinee today. Come to Nero Wolfe's office at half past two. Six-eighteen West Thirty-fifth Street. Your cigarette case will be there, and you can settle it with Mr. Wolfe."

"But why can't you—"

"No. That's how it is, and I have things to do." I put a hand out. "The keys."

"Why can't I—"

"I said no. There's no argument and no time. Damn it, I'm giving you a break. The keys."

She opened her bag, fingered in it, took out a leather key fold, and handed it over. I unsnapped it, saw two Rabson keys, which are not like any others, displayed them to Perez, and asked if they were the keys to the door and the elevator. He took a look and said yes. Dropping them in a pocket, I pushed the button to open the elevator door and told Meg Duncan, "I'll see you later. Half past two."

"Why can't I stay until you find—"

"Nothing doing. I'll be too busy for company."

She stepped in, the door closed, the click came, and the faint sound. I turned to Perez.

"You've never seen her before."

"No. Never."

"Phooey. When you brought things up at midnight?"

"I only saw him. She could have been in the bathroom."

"Where's the bathroom?"

He pointed. "At that end."

I went to his wife. "When she saw you she said, 'Thank God it's you.'"

She nodded. "I heard her. She must see me some time when she came in, in the hall or a door was open. We don't know her. We never saw her."

"The things you don't know. All right now, you two. It will take hours and will have to wait because I have things to do, but one question now." To him: "When you put the body in the hole why did you climb in and put the tarp over it?"

He was surprised. "But he was dead! A man dead, you cover him! I knew that thing was in there, I had seen it."

That was the moment that I decided that Cesar Perez had not killed Thomas G. Yeager. Possibly his wife had, but not him. If you had been there looking at him as he said that, you would have decided the same. When I had been trying to account for the tarp the simplest explanation had never occurred to me, that long ago people covered dead men to hide them from vultures, and it got to be a habit.

"That was decent," I said. "Too bad you didn't wear gloves. Okay, that's all for now. I have work to do. You heard me give that woman Nero Wolfe's address, Six-eighteen West Thirty-fifth Street. Be there at six o'clock this afternoon, both of you. I'm your detective temporarily, but he's the boss. You certainly need help, and after you tell him about it we'll see. Where are Yeager's keys? Don't say 'We don't know.' You said you took them. Where are they?"

"I have them safe," Mrs. Perez said.

"Where?"

"In a cake. I made a cake and put them in. There are twelve keys in a thing."

"Including the keys to the door and the elevator?"

"Yes."

I considered. I was already on thin ice, and if I took possession of something that had been taken from Yeager's body there would be no ice at all between me and suppression of evidence. No. "Don't cut the cake," I said, "and be darned sure nobody else does. Are you going anywhere today? Either of you?"

"We don't have to," she said.

"Then don't. Nero Wolfe's office at six o'clock, but I'll see you when I come down, probably in an hour or so."

"You take things?"

"I don't know. If I do I'll show them to you, including the cigarette case. If I take anything you think I shouldn't, you can call in that cop from out front."

"We couldn't," Perez said.

"He makes a joke," she told him. She pushed the button to bring the elevator up. "This is a bad day, Cesar. There will be many bad days, and he makes a joke." The elevator clicked at the top, she pushed another button, the door opened, and they entered and were gone.

I moved my eyes around. At the edge of a panel of red silk at the left was a rectangular brass plate, if it wasn't gold. I went and pulled on it, and it gave.

The panel was a door. I pushed it open and stepped through, and was in the kitchen. The walls were red tile, the cupboards and shelves were yellow plastic, and the sink and appliances, including the refrigerator and electric range, were stainless steel. I opened the refrigerator door, saw a collection of various items, and closed it. I slid a cupboard door back and saw nine bottles of Dom Pérignon champagne on their sides in a plastic rack. That would do for the kitchen for now. I emerged and walked the length of the yellow carpet, surrounded by silk and skin, to the other end, where there was another brass plate, or gold, at the edge of a panel. I pushed it open and was in the bathroom. I don't know what your taste is, but I liked it. It was all mirrors and marble, red marble with yellow streaks and splotches. The tub, big enough for two, was the same marble. Two of the mirrors were doors to cabinets, and they contained enough different cosmetic items to supply a harem.

I returned to the silk and skin. There were no drawers anywhere, no piece of furniture that might contain pieces of paper on which someone had written something. There was nothing at the telephone stand but the phone, which was yellow, and the directory, which was in a red leather holder. But along one wall, the one across from the bed, there was no furniture for about thirty feet of its length, and the silk along the bottom, for three feet up from the floor, was in little folds like a curtain, not flat as it was everywhere else. I went and gave the silk a tug and it parted and slid along the top, and behind it were drawer fronts, of wood something like mahogany, but redder. I pulled one open. Female slippers, a dozen pairs in two neat rows, various colors and shapes and sizes. The sizes ranged from quite small to fairly large.

I looked into only five more drawers before I went to the phone. That was enough to make it plain that Meg Duncan wasn't the only one who had keys to the door and elevator. There was another drawer of slippers, again assorted colors and sizes, and two drawers of nighties, a mighty fine collection. It was after I unfolded eight of them and spread them on the bed for comparison, and found that they also covered a wide range in sizes, that I went to the phone and dialed a number. There was a possibility that it was tapped or there was an extension, but it was very slim, and I preferred the slight risk to going out to a booth.

Saul Panzer, whose number I dialed, was the free-lance operative we called on when only the best would do. But what I got was the answering-service girl, who said that Mr. Panzer was out and couldn't be reached and would I leave a message. I said no and dialed another number, Fred Durkin's, the next best, and got him. He said he had nothing on for the day.

"You have now," I told him. "Pack a bag for a week. It will probably be less but could be more. Come as you are, no costumes required, but have a gun. You probably won't use it, but have it. Come to One-fifty-six West Eighty-second Street, the basement entrance, superintendent, and push the button at the door. It will be a man or a woman, either Cuban or Puerto Rican, I'm not sure which. They speak American. Tell him or her your name and ask for me, and you'll have the pleasure and honor of being brought to my presence. Don't hurry. Take three minutes to pack if you want to."

"Eighty-second Street," he said. "Murder. What was his name? Yeager."

· "You read too much and you're morbid and you jump to conclusions. Pack your bag and button your lip." I hung up.

Folding flimsy nighties properly is no job for a man and it takes time, but I gritted my teeth and stuck to it, because a detective is supposed to leave a place the way he found it. Them back in the drawer, I brought the elevator up, took it down, and went to an open door, the first one on the left in the hall. The Perez family was having a conference in the kitchen. Father and mother were sitting, and Maria was standing. There was more light than there had been in the front of the hall, and with that rare specimen, the more light the better. Looking at her, any man alive would have the thought, What the hell, I could wash the dishes and darn the socks myself. The beige nightie with lace around the top, medium-sized, would have fitted her fine. I made my eyes go to her parents and spoke.

"A man will come pretty soon, tall and thick in all directions. He'll give his name, Fred Durkin, and ask for me. Send him up."

I got the expected reaction from Mrs. Perez. I had no right to tell anybody about that place, they were going to pay me, and so forth. Wishing to keep on speaking terms with our clients, I took four minutes to explain why I had to leave Fred there when I went, got her calmed down, permitted my eyes to dart another glance at Maria, took the elevator back up, and resumed on the drawers where I had left off. I won't take time and space to list an inventory, but will merely say that every-thing that could be needed for such an establishment was there. I'll only mention two details: one, that there was only one drawer of male items, and the six suits of pajamas were all the same size; and two, the drawer in which I found Meg Duncan's cigarette case was obviously a catchall. There were three women's handkerchiefs, used, an anonymous compact, a lady's umbrella, a matchbook from Terry's Pub, and other such miscellany. I had just put it all back in and was closing the drawer when I heard the click from the elevator.

Presumably it was Fred, but possibly not, so I got the Marley out and went to the wall by the elevator door. I could hear no voices from below; the place was so thoroughly soundproofed that you could hear nothing but a faint suggestion of noise from the street traffic, and that was more felt than heard. Soon the click came again, the door opened, and Fred slipped out. He stood and swiveled his head, right and left, brought it around until he caught a glimpse of me, turned it back again, and spoke.

"Jesus Kee-rist!"

"Your new home," I told him. "I do hope you'll be happy here. The idea is, you take your pick from the pictures. Something like the Mountain Room at the Churchill with live trout and you choose the one you want for lunch. I strongly recommend the one over there sitting on a rose bush. If she can stand thorns she can stand you."

He put his bag down. "You know, Archie, I've always wondered why you didn't marry. How long have you had it?"

"Oh, ten years, I guess. I have others here and there around town. I'm turning this one over to you for a while. Kitchen, bathroom, TV, maid service. Like it?"

"Good God. I'm a married man."

"Yeah. Too bad. I'd like to stay and explain the pictures to you, but I have to go. The point is, if a visitor comes, someone should be here to receive her. It could be a him, but more likely it would be a her. Most likely there won't be any, but there might be. She might come at any hour, day or night. The less you know the better; just take my word for it that if she steps out of that elevator you are in a position to refuse to let her get back in, and there's no other way out of here. Identify yourself or not, as you prefer. Ring me, and I'll come."

He was frowning. "Alone with a woman, restraining her by force isn't so good."

"You won't have to touch her unless she starts it."

"She sticks her head out a window and yells police."

"Not a chance. There's no window, and she wouldn't want anyone to know she's here, least of all a cop. The one thing she'll want is to get out, and fast."

He was still frowning. "The hole that Yeager's body was found in is right out front. Maybe I ought to know a little more."

"Not from me. Why drag in Yeager? He's dead; I read it in the paper. If the phone rings take it and ask who it is and see what happens, but don't say who you are. That's the door to the kitchen." I pointed. "There's some fancy stuff in the refrigerator when you get hungry. The people down below are Mr. and Mrs. Cesar Perez and their daughter Maria. Did you see Maria?"

"No."

"I'm going to marry her when I find time. I'll tell Mrs. Perez to bring you up a loaf of bread, and if you have to have anything she'll get it. She and her husband are out on a limb and they're counting on me to get a ladder. Okay, enjoy the pictures. You couldn't ask for a better chance to study anatomy." I opened the elevator door.

"What if it's a man that comes?"

"It won't be. If it is, stick to the program; that's why I told you to have a gun."

"What if it's a cop?"

"One chance in a million. Not even that. Tell him you've forgotten your name and he'll have to ring me at Nero Wolfe's office. Then I'll know what happened."

"And I'll be in the coop."

"Right. But not for long. We'll have you out by Christmas easy. There's half a pound of fresh caviar in the refrigerator, twenty dollars' worth. Help yourself."

I entered the elevator. Downstairs I explained the situation to Mrs. Perez and asked her to take up a loaf of bread, and left the house. My watch said noon, on the dot, as I headed for Columbus Avenue for a taxi.

Chapter 5

At five minutes past one, Wolfe, at his desk, growled at me. "Your objective was to find an acceptable client, not a pair of wretches who probably killed him and another wretch who offers a reward for a cigarette case. I concede your craft, your finesse, and your gumption, and I even felicitate you, but if you have discovered the culprits, as seems probable, where do you send a bill?"

I had reported in full, omitting only one detail, a factual description of Maria. He was quite capable of assuming, or pretending to assume, that I was prejudiced in favor of Mr. and Mrs. Perez on account of their daughter. I had described the place accurately and completely, and had even included my handling of the nightie problem. I had admitted that I had tried to get Saul Panzer (ten dollars an hour), and had got Fred Durkin instead (seven-fifty an hour) only because Saul was not available.

"I won't see them," he said.

I knew, or thought I did, where the real snag was, but I had to go easy. I nodded thoughtfully. "Of course they could have killed him," I said, "but one will get you five that they didn't. For the reasons I gave. His tone and his expression when he told me why he put the tarp over the body. The fact that she let the daughter come to the door when I rang the bell. If she had killed him she would have come herself. But chiefly, with him alive they were in clover. Of course he was paying them plenty. With him dead they're not only minus a fat income, they're in a hell of a fix, and they would have been even if I hadn't got to them. When the executor of his estate learns that he owned that house and goes to inspect it?"

I crossed my legs. "Naturally," I said, "you don't like it, I understand that. If it was just a nice place he had fixed up where he could safely spend a night now and then with his mistress, that wouldn't be so bad, but obviously it wasn't that. There are probably half a dozen women with keys to that door and elevator, and maybe twenty or more. I realize that you wouldn't like to be involved with that kind of setup, but now that I have—"

"Nonsense," he said.

I raised a brow. "Nonsense?"

"Yes. A modern satyr is part man, part pig, and part jackass. He hasn't even the charm of the roguish; he doesn't lean gracefully against a tree with a flute in his hand. The only quality he has preserved from his Attic ancestors is his lust, and he gratifies it in dark corners or other men's beds or hotel rooms, not in the shade of an olive tree on a sunny hillside. The preposterous blower of carnality you have described is a sorry makeshift, but at least Mr. Yeager tried. A pig and a jackass, yes, but the flute strain was in him too—as it once was in me, in my youth. No doubt he deserved to die, but I would

welcome a sufficient inducement to expose his
killer."

I suppose I was staring. "You would?"

"Certainly. But who is likely to offer it? Granting that you have shown commendable alacrity and
wit, and that you are right about Mr. and Mrs.
Perez, where are we? Where is a prospective client?
To whom can we disclose the existence of that
preposterous bower and his connection with it?
Neither his family nor his business associates,
surely. They would be more likely to want it con-
cealed than disclosed, and are we blackmailers? I
concede that there is one remote possibility: who is
the man who came here yesterday posing as Yeager, and why did he come?"

I shook my head. "Sorry I can't oblige. Have you
read my report?"

"Yes. Manifestly he is a man with a special and
educated fondness for words. He said, 'Else there
was no use coming.' He said, 'I can speak in assured
confidence?' He said, 'That will suffice.' The last two
are merely noticeable, but the first is extraordinary.
'Else' instead of 'or' or 'otherwise'? Remarkable."

"If you say so."

"I do. But also, merely talking along, he quoted
from John Webster's *The Duchess of Malfi*: 'Other
sins only speak; murder shrieks out.' He quoted
from John Harington's *Alcilia*: 'Treason doth never
prosper.' He quoted from Browning's *Paracelsus*:
'Measure your mind's height by the shade it casts.'
People quote to display their erudition, but why to
you? You heard him and were looking at him. Was
he trying to impress you?"

"No. He was talking, that was all."

"Just so. And he had sentences at the tip of his

tongue from two Elizabethans and Robert Browning. Not one man in ten thousand is familiar with both Webster and Browning. He's a pedagogue. He's a teacher of literature."

"You're not."

"I recognized only Webster. I looked up the others. I don't know Harington, and Browning repels me. So he is one in ten thousand, and there are less than a thousand of him in New York. I invite a trial of your ingenuity: if he knew Yeager was dead, either because he had killed him or otherwise, why did he come here with that tarra-diddle?"

"I pass. I've already tried it, last night. If he had killed him, the only possibility was that he was cracked, and he wasn't. If he hadn't killed him but knew he was dead, the best I could do was that he wanted to call attention to that block on Eighty-second Street and that house, and to buy that I'd have to be cracked myself. An anonymous phone call to the police would have been quicker and simpler. Can you do any better?"

"No. No one can. He did not know Yeager was dead. Then, thinking Yeager alive, what did he hope to accomplish by that masquerade? He could not assume with confidence that when Yeager failed to appear you would either telephone his house or go there, but he knew that before long, either last evening or this morning, you would communicate with him, you would learn that your caller was an impostor, and you would tell Yeager about it. With what result? Merely that Yeager would know what the impostor had told you. If he identified the impostor from your description, he would know that that man knew of his visits to the Eighty-second

Street address, but I reject that. If the impostor
wanted Yeager to know *who* knew about that house,
why all the fuss of coming to you? Why not just tell
him, by phone or mail or face-to-face, or even in an
anonymous note? No. He knew that Yeager would
not identify him from your description. He merely
wanted Yeager to know that *someone* knew of his
connection with that house, and possibly also that
you and I now knew about it. So I doubt if he could
or would be helpful, but all the same I would like to
speak with him."

"So would I. That was one reason I got Fred
there. There's a bare chance that he has keys and
will show up."

Wolfe grunted. "Pfui. The chance that anyone at
all will come there is minute and you know it. You
got Fred there because I cannot now say merely
that the incident is closed. I would have to tell you
to recall him, and you know that I respect your
commitments as I do my own. Yes, Fritz?"

"Lunch is ready, sir. The parsley had wilted and
I used chives."

"We'll see." Wolfe pushed his chair back and
arose. "Pepper?"

"No, sir. I thought not, with chives."

"I agree, but we'll see."

I followed him out and across the hall to the
dining room. As we finished the clam juice Fritz
came with the first installment of dumplings, four
apiece. Some day I would like to see how long I can
keep going on Fritz's marrow dumplings, of
chopped beef marrow, bread crumbs, parsley
(chives today), grated lemon rind, salt, and eggs,
boiled four minutes in strong meat stock. If he
boiled them all at once of course they would get

mushy after the first eight or ten, but he does them eight at a time, and they keep coming. They are one of the few dishes with which I stay neck and neck with Wolfe clear to the tape, and they were the reason I had let it pass when he had said he wouldn't see the clients I had got. Those marrow dumplings induce a state of mind in which anybody would see anybody. And it worked. We had finished the salad and returned to the office, and Fritz had brought coffee, when the doorbell rang. I went to the hall for a look through the one-way glass, stepped back in, and told Wolfe, "Meg Duncan. At least we might as well collect for the cigarette case. Say two bucks?"

He glared. "Confound you." He put his cup down. "What if she killed him? Does that concern us? Very well, you invited her. Five minutes."

I went to the front and opened the door. It wasn't a thirty-year-old female with a good enough face, in a plain gray suit and a plain little hat, who gave me a smile that would warm a glacier as she crossed the sill. The face had been arranged by a professional and was being handled by a professional, and while the dress and jacket were not spectacular they were by no means plain. And the voice was the voice of an angel who might consider taking a week off if she got an invitation that appealed to her. Not only did she use it on me in the hall, but also on Wolfe when I steered her to the office and he stood, inclined his head an eighth of an inch, and indicated the red leather chair.

Her smile was on full. Granting that it was professional, it was a damned good smile. "I know how busy you men are with important things," she said, "so I won't take your time." To me: "Did you find it?"

"He did," Wolfe said. He sat. "Sit down, Miss Duncan. I like eyes at my level. A brief discussion may be necessary. If you answer two or three questions satisfactorily you may have the cigarette case when you have paid me fifty thousand dollars."

The smile went. "Fifty *thousand*? That's fantastic!"

"Sit down, please."

She looked at me, saw merely a working detective, moved to the red leather chair, sat on the edge, and said, "Of course you don't mean that. You can't."

Wolfe, leaning back, regarded her. "I do and I don't. Our position—I include Mr. Goodwin—is peculiar and a little delicate. The body of a man who had died by violence was found in that hole on that street near that house. He was a man of means and standing. The police don't know of his connection with that house and his quarters there, but we do, and we intend to use that knowledge to our profit. I don't suppose you are familiar with the statutes regarding suppression of evidence of a crime. It may even—"

"My cigarette case isn't evidence of a crime!"

"I haven't said it is. It may even lead to a charge of accessory to murder. Interpretation of that statute is in some respects vague, but not in others. Knowingly concealing or disposing of a tangible object that would help to identify the criminal or convict him would of course be suppression of evidence; but words may be evidence or may not. Usually not. If you were to tell me now that you entered that room Sunday night, found Yeager's body there, and got Mr. Perez to help you take it from the house and put it in that hole, that would not be evidence. I couldn't be successfully prosecuted if I failed to tell the police what you had told me; I would merely swear that I thought you were lying."

She had slid back in the chair a little. "I wasn't in that room Sunday night."

"Not evidence. You may be lying. I'm only explaining the delicacy of our position. You told Mr. Goodwin you would pay him a thousand dollars to find your cigarette case and keep it for you, and give it to you later at his discretion. We can't accept that offer. It would engage us not to turn it over to the police even if it became apparent that it would help to identify or convict a murderer, and that's too great a risk for a thousand dollars. You may have it for fifty thousand, cash or a certified check. Do you want it?"

I *think* he meant it. I think he would have handed it over for thirty grand, or even twenty, if she had been dumb enough to pay it. He had let me go up to 82nd Street with five Cs in my pocket for one specific reason, to see if I could flush a prospect for a worthy fee, and if she was fool enough, or desperate enough, to pay twenty grand, not to mention fifty, for her cigarette case, he could call it a day and leave the murder investigation to the law. As for the risk, he had taken bigger ones. He was saying only that he would give her the case, not that he would forget about it.

She was staring at him. "I didn't think," she said, "that Nero Wolfe was a blackmailer."

"Neither does the dictionary, madam." He swiveled to the stand that had held the three Websters he had worn out and now held a new one. Opening it and finding the page, he read: 'Payment of money exacted by means of intimidation; also, extortion of money from a person by threats of public accusation, exposure, or censure.'" He swiveled back. "I don't fit. I haven't threatened or intimidated you."

"But you . . ." She looked at me and back to him. "Where would I get fifty thousand dollars? You might as well say a million. What are you going to do? Are you going to give it to the police?"

"Not by choice. Only under the compulsion of circumstance. A factor would be your answers to my questions."

"You haven't asked me any questions."

"I do now. Were you in that room Sunday evening or night?"

"No." Her chin was up.

"When were you last there? Before today."

"I haven't said I was ever there."

"That's egregious. Your behavior this morning. Your offer to Mr. Goodwin. You had keys. When?"

She set her teeth on her lip. Five seconds. "More than a week ago. A week ago Saturday. That's when I left the cigarette case. Oh my God." She extended a hand, not a professional gesture. "Mr. Wolfe, this could ruin my career. I haven't seen him since that night. I don't know who killed him, or why, or anything. Why must you drag me into it? What good will it do?"

"I didn't drag you there this morning, madam. I don't ask how often you visited that room because your answer would be worthless, but when you did visit were others there?"

"No."

"Was anyone ever there when you were besides Mr. Yeager?"

"No. Never."

"But other women went there. That's not surmise, it's established. Of course you knew that; Mr.
Yeager was not concerned to conceal it. Who are
they?"

"I don't know."

"You don't deny that you knew there were
others?"

She thought she was going to, but his eyes had
her pinned. She swallowed the yes and said, "No. I
knew that."

"Of course. He wanted you to. His arrangement
for keeping slippers and garments testifies that he
derived pleasure not only from his present compan-
ion but also from her awareness that she had—
uh—colleagues. Or rivals. So surely he wasn't
silent about them? Surely he spoke of them, in
comparison, in praise or derogation? And if he
didn't name them he must have aroused conjecture.
This is my most instant question, Miss Duncan: who
are they?"

I had heard Wolfe ask questions of women that
made them tremble, or turn pale, or yell at him, or
burst into tears, or fly at him, but that was the first
time I ever heard one that made a woman blush—
and her a sophisticated Broadway star. I suppose it
was his matter-of-fact way of putting it. I didn't
blush, but I cleared my throat. She not only
blushed; she lowered her head and shut her eyes.

"Naturally," Wolfe said, "you would like this
episode to pass into history as quickly as possible. It
might help if you will tell me something about the
others."

"I can't." She raised her head. The blush was

gone. "I don't know anything about them. Are you going to keep my cigarette case?"

"For the present, yes."

"You have me at your mercy." She started to rise, found that her knees were shaky, and put a hand on the chair arm to help. She got erect. "I was a fool to go there, an utter fool. I could have said—I could have said anything. I could have said I lost it. What a fool." She looked at me straight, said, "I wish I had clawed your eyes out," turned, and headed for the door. I got up and followed her, passed her in the hall, and had the front door open when she reached it. She wasn't very steady on her feet, so I watched her descend the seven steps to the sidewalk before I shut the door and returned to the office. Wolfe was in his reading position and had opened his book, *An Outline of Man's Knowledge of the Modern World*, edited by Lyman Bryson. I had spent an hour one afternoon looking it over, and had seen nothing about modern satyrs.

Chapter 6

Six years ago, reporting one of Wolfe's cases, one in which no fee or hope of one was involved, I tried a stunt that I got good and tired of before I was through. It took us to Montenegro, and nearly all the talk was in a language I didn't know a word of, but I got enough of it out of Wolfe later to report it verbatim. I'm not going to repeat that experience, so I'll merely give you the gist of his conversation with Mr. and Mrs. Perez when he came down from the plant rooms at six o'clock and found them there. It was in Spanish. Either he took the opportunity to speak one of his six languages, or he thought they would be freer in their native tongue, or he wanted to rile me, I don't know which. Probably all three. After they had gone he gave me the substance.

This isn't evidence; it's just what they said. They didn't know who came Sunday evening, man or woman, or how many, or when he or she or they had left. They didn't know how many different people came at different times. Sometimes they had heard footsteps in the hall, and they had always sounded like women. If a man had ever come they hadn't seen or heard him. No one had ever been in the room when they went up to clean; they didn't go up if the elevator was up there, but that had happened only five or six times in four years.

They had heard no shot Sunday evening, but even the floor of the room was soundproofed. When Perez went up at midnight there had been a smell of burnt powder, but he thought it was a weak smell and she thought it was a strong one. There had been nothing in the room that didn't belong there—no gun, no coat or hat or wrap. Yeager had been fully dressed; his hat and topcoat had been on a chair, and they had put them in the hole with the body. None of the slippers or garments or other articles were out of the drawers. The bed had not been disturbed. Everything was in place in the bathroom. They had taken nothing from Yeager's body but his keys. They had cleaned the room Monday morning, vacuumed and dusted, but had taken nothing out of it.

They had paid no rent for their basement. Yeager had paid them fifty dollars a week and had let them keep the rent they collected for the rooms on the four floors. Their total take had been around two hundred dollars a week (probably nearer three hundred and maybe more). They had no reason to suppose that Yeager had left them the house, or anything else, in his will. They were sure that none of the tenants had any connection with Yeager or knew anything about him; the renting had been completely in their hands. They had decided that one hundred dollars wasn't enough to pay Wolfe and me, and though it would take most of their savings (this isn't evidence) they thought five hundred would be better, and they had brought half of that amount along. Of course Wolfe didn't take it. He told them that while he had no present intention of passing on any of the information they had given him he had to be free to use his discretion. That started an argument. Since it was in Spanish I can't give it blow by blow, but judging from the tones and expressions, and from the fact that at one point Mrs. Perez was up and at Wolfe's desk, slapping it, it got pretty warm. She had calmed down some by the time they left.

Since they didn't leave until dinnertime and business is barred at the table, Wolfe didn't relay it to me until we were back in the office after dinner. When he had finished he said, "It's bootless. Time, effort, and money wasted. That woman killed him. Call Fred." He picked up his book.

"Sure," I said, "no question about it. It was such a nuisance, all that money rolling in, three hundred a week or more, she had to put a stop to it, and that was the easiest way, shoot him and dump him in a hole."

He shook his head. "She is a creature of passion. You saw her face when I asked if her daughter had ever gone up to that room—no, you didn't know what I had asked her. Her eyes blazed, and her voice shrilled. She discovered that Yeager had debauched her daughter and she killed him. Call Fred."

"She admitted it?"

"Certainly not. She said that her daughter had been forbidden to go up to that room and had never seen it. She resented the implication with fury. We are no longer concerned." He opened the book. "Call Fred."

"I don't believe it." My voice may have shrilled slightly. "I haven't described Maria at length and

don't intend to, but when I start marrying she will
be third on the list and might even be first if I didn't
have prior commitments. She may be part witch but
she has not been debauched. If and when she orgies
with a satyr he'll be leaning gracefully against a
tree with a flute in his hand. I don't believe it."

"Orgy is not a verb."

"It is now. And when I asked you this morning if
there was any limit to how much I should take along
and disburse if necessary, you said as dictated by
my discretion and sagacity. I took five hundred, and
my discretion and sagacity dictated that the best
way to use it was to get Fred there and keep him
there. Sixty hours at seven-fifty an hour is four
hundred and fifty dollars. Add fifty for his grub and
incidentals and that's the five hundred. The sixty
hours will be up at eleven-thirty p.m. Thursday, day
after tomorrow. Since I have met Maria and you
haven't, and since you left it—"

The phone rang. I whirled my chair and got it.
"Nero Wolfe's reside—"

"Archie! I've got one."

"Man or woman?"

"Woman. You coming?"

"Immediately. You'll be seeing me." I cradled
the phone and stood up. "Fred has caught a fish.
Female." I glanced at the wall clock: a quarter to
ten. "I can have her here before eleven, maybe by
ten-thirty. Instructions?"

He exploded. "What good would it do," he
roared, "to give you instructions?"

I could have challenged him to name one time
when I had failed to follow instructions unless
forced by circumstances, but with a genius you have
to be tactful. I said merely, "Then I'll use my

discretion and sagacity," and went. I should have
used them in the hall, to stop at the rack for my
topcoat, as I discovered when I was out and headed
for Tenth Avenue. A cold wind, cold for May, was
coming from the river, but I didn't go back. Getting
a taxi at the corner, I told the driver 82nd and
Amsterdam. There might still be a cop at the hole,
and even if there wasn't it would be just as well not
to take a cab right to the door.

There was no cop at the hole, and no gathering
of amateur criminologists, just passers-by and a
bunch of teen-agers down the block. After turning
in at 156, descending the three steps, and using Meg
Duncan's key, I entered and proceeded down the
hall; and halfway along I had a feeling. Someone had
an eye on me. Of course that experience, feeling a
presence you have neither seen nor heard, is as old
as rocks, but it always gets you. I get it at the
bottom of my spine, showing perhaps that I would
be either raising or lowering my tail if I had one. At
the moment I had the feeling there was a door three
paces ahead of me on the right, opened to a crack, a
bare inch. I kept going, and when I reached the
door I shot an arm out and pushed it. It swung in a
foot and was stopped, but the foot was enough.
There was no light inside and the hall was dim, but
I have good eyes.

She didn't move. "Why did you do that?" she
asked. "This is my room." A remarkable thing; with
a strong light on her, that was best, and with a dim
one, *that* was best.

"I beg your pardon," I said. "As you know, I'm a
detective, and detectives have bad habits. How
many times have you been in the room on the top
floor?"

"I'm not allowed," she said. "Would I tell you? So you could tell my mother? Excuse me, I shut the door."

She did, and I didn't block it. A nice long talk with her would be desirable, but it would have to wait. I went to the elevator and used the other key, stepped in, and was lifted.

You have expectations even when you're not aware of them. I suppose I was expecting to find a scared or indignant female sitting on a couch or chair and Fred near at hand with an eye on her. It wasn't like that. Fred was standing in the center of the room holding up his pants, with two red streaks down his cheek. For a second I thought she wasn't there; then I saw her head sticking out of the bundle on the floor. It was the yellow silk coverlet from the bed, and she was wrapped in it, with Fred's belt strapped around the middle. I went and looked down at her, and she glared up at me.

"She's not hurt any," Fred said. "I wish she was. Look at me."

The red of the streaks on his cheek was blood. He lifted a hand with a handkerchief and dabbed at it. "You said I wouldn't have to touch her unless she started it. She started it all right. Then when I went for the phone she went for the elevator, and when I went to head her off she went for the phone. So I had to wrap her up."

"Have you told her who you are?"

"No. I wouldn't do her that favor. That's her bag there." He pointed to a chair. "I haven't looked in it."

A voice came from the bundle on the floor. "Who are you?" it demanded.

I ignored her and went and got the bag and

opened it. With the other usual items, it contained four that were helpful: credit cards from three stores and a driver's license. The name was Julia McGee, with an address on Arbor Street in the Village. She was twenty-nine years old, five feet five inches, white, brown hair and brown eyes. I put the stuff back in the bag and the bag on the chair, and went to her.

"I'll unwrap you in a minute, Miss McGee," I said. "His name is Fred Durkin and mine is Archie Goodwin. You may have heard of Nero Wolfe, the private detective. We work for him. Mr. Durkin is camped here because Mr. Wolfe wants to have a talk with anyone who comes to this room. I'll be glad to take you to him. I ask no questions because I'd only have to tell him what you said, and it will be simpler to let him ask them."

"Let me up!" she demanded.

"In a minute. Now that I know who you are and where to find you the situation is a little different. If you grab your bag and head for the elevator I won't try to stop you, but I advise you to count to ten first. There are keys in your bag to the door downstairs and the elevator. If and when the police get to this room they will of course be interested in anyone who had keys and could have been here Sunday night. So it might be a mistake to decline my invitation. Think it over while I'm unwrapping you."

I squatted to unbuckle the belt and pull it from under her, and Fred came and took it. I couldn't stand her up to unwrap her because her feet were inside too. "The easiest way," I told her, "is to roll out while I hold the end." She rolled. That thing was ten feet square, and I never have asked Fred how he managed it. When she was out she bounced up and was on her feet. She was quite attractive, perhaps more than normally with her face flushed and her hair tousled. She shook herself, yanked her coat around into place, went and got her bag, and said, "I'm going to phone."

"Not here," I told her. "If you're leaving alone, there's a booth at the corner. If you're going with me, there's a phone in Mr. Wolfe's office."

She looked more mad than scared, but that's always a guess with a strange face. "Do you know whose room this is?" she demanded.

"I know whose it was. Thomas G. Yeager's."

"What are you doing here?"

"Skip it. I not only won't ask questions, I won't answer them."

"You have no right . . ." She let that go. "I am Mr. Yeager's secretary. I was. I came to get a notebook I left here, that's all."

"Then you have nothing to fear. If and when the police get to you, just tell them that and they'll apologize for bothering you."

"If I don't go with you, you're going to tell the police?"

"I haven't said so. Mr. Wolfe makes the decisions. I'm just the errand boy."

She moved. I thought she was bound for the phone, but she kept straight on, to the far end, to the door to the bathroom, and on through. I went and took a look at Fred's cheek. He had his belt back on. "So this was Yeager's room," he said. "Now since I know that—"

"You don't. You don't know anything. I lied to her and she fell for it. Your job is merely to be here to welcome callers. There's no harm done. Your cheek looks worse than it is, and there's stuff in the bathroom for it. You would have had to take the coverlet off anyway when you go to bed. I'll help you fold it."

I took one end and he took the other. He asked how long he would have to hang on there, and I said until further notice, and what better could he ask? Any man with a feeling for the finer things of life would consider it a privilege to be allowed to shack up in such an art gallery as that, and he was getting paid for it, twenty-four hours a day. He said even the TV had caught it; when he turned it on what he had got was a woman in a bathtub blowing soap bubbles.

As he put the folded coverlet on a couch Julia McGee reappeared. She had adjusted the neck of her dress, put her hair in order, and repaired her face. She wasn't at all bad-looking. She came up to me and said, "All right, I'm accepting your invitation."

Chapter 7

When you enter the hall of the old brownstone on West 35th Street, the first door on your left is to what we call the front room, and the one beyond it is to the office. Both of those rooms are soundproofed, not as perfectly as Yeager's bower of carnality, but well enough, including the doors. I took Julia McGee to the front room, had my offer to take her coat declined, and went through the connecting door to the office, closing it behind me. Wolfe was in his favorite chair with his book. He is not a fast reader, and that book has 667 pages, with about 600 words to the page. When I crossed to his desk and told him I had brought company he finished a paragraph, closed the book on a finger, and scowled at me.

I went on. "Her name is Julia McGee. She says she was Yeager's secretary, which is probably true because it can be easily checked. She says she went there tonight to get a notebook she had left there, which is a lie and not a very good one. There is no notebook in that room. When she entered and saw Fred she went for him and drew blood on his face, and he had to wrap her up in a bed cover so he could use the phone. After I got her name and address from things in her bag I told her she could either go now and explain to the police later or she could come here with me, and she came with me. I made a concession, I told her she could use the phone as soon as she got here, with us present."

He said, "Grrrrh." I gave him two seconds to add to it, but apparently that was all, so I went and opened the door to the front room and told her to come in. She came on by me, stopped to glance around, saw the phone on my desk, crossed to it, sat in my chair, and dialed. Wolfe inserted his bookmark, put the book down, leaned back, and glared at her.

She told the receiver, "I want to speak to Mr. Aiken. This is Julia McGee. . . . That's right. . . . Thank you." A one-minute wait. "Mr. Aiken? . . . Yes. . . . Yes, I know, but I had to tell you, there was a man there and he attacked me and . . . . No, let me tell you, another man came and said they were working for Nero Wolfe, the detective. . . . Yes, Nero Wolfe. The second one, Archie Goodwin, said Nero Wolfe wanted to talk with anyone who came to that room and wanted me to go with him, and that's where I am now, in Nero Wolfe's office. . . . Yes. . . . No, I don't think so, they're both right here, Nero Wolfe and Archie Goodwin. . . . I don't know. . . . Yes, of course, but I don't know. . . . Wait, I'll ask."

She turned to me. "What's this address?" I told her, and she went back to the phone. "Six-eighteen West Thirty-fifth Street. . . . That's right. . . . Yes, I will." She hung up, swiveled, told Wolfe, "Mr. Aiken will be here in twenty minutes," and wriggled her coat off.

Wolfe asked, "Who is Mr. Aiken?"

Her look was what you would get from the Yankee batboy if you asked him who is Mr. Stengel. "Mr. Benedict Aiken. The president of Continental Plastic Products."

That changed my mind. Wanting my own chair, I had been about to move her to the red leather one, but she would only have to move again when the president came, so I brought one of the yellow ones for her, facing Wolfe's desk, and put her coat on the couch. As she changed to it Wolfe lifted his head to sniff. His opinion of perfume may be only a part of his opinion of women. He always thinks he smells it when there's a woman in the room. I had been closer to Julia McGee than he had, and she wasn't scented.

He eyed her. "You told Mr. Goodwin that you went to that room this evening to get a notebook you had left there. When did you leave it?"

She was meeting his eyes. "I'll wait until Mr. Aiken gets here."

Wolfe shook his head. "That won't do. I can't prevent his coming, but he'll enter only if it suits me. I want some facts before he arrives. When did you leave the notebook?"

She opened her mouth and closed it again. In a moment she spoke. "I didn't. That was a—that wasn't true. I went there this evening because Mr. Aiken asked me to."

"Indeed. To get something he had left?"

"No. I'd rather wait until he's here, but it doesn't matter. You know that place was Mr. Yeager's, so it doesn't matter. Mr. Aiken sent me there to see if there was anything there that would connect Mr. Yeager with it, that would show it was his place."

"Mr. Aiken gave you keys?"

"No, I had keys. I had been there a few times to take dictation from Mr. Yeager. I was his secretary."

Wolfe grunted. "I haven't seen that room, but Mr. Goodwin has described it. Did you think it a suitable milieu for business dictation?"

"It wasn't my place to think it was suitable or wasn't. If he thought it was—he was my boss."

Wolfe looked at me. I raised my brows. One brow up meant no, even money. Two brows up meant no, five to one. He returned to her.

"If you had found something that showed it was Mr. Yeager's place, what were you going to do with it?"

"I was going to take it. Take it away."

"As instructed by Mr. Aiken?"

"Yes."

"Why?"

"Mr. Aiken can tell you that better than I can."

"You must have a notion. You didn't think that he was merely indulging a whim."

"Of course not. The obvious reason was that he wanted to protect the reputation of Continental Plastic Products. It was bad enough, the executive vice-president being murdered. Mr. Aiken didn't want it to be known that he had been—that he had had a—a place like that."

"Do you know how Mr. Aiken found out that Mr. Yeager had that place?"

"Yes. I told him."

"When?"

"About two months ago. Mr. Yeager had had me go there twice—no, three times—to take dictation in the evening. He said he could think better, do better work, away from the office. Of course you're right, what you said about that room. I thought it was very—well, vulgar for him to ask me to go there. I worried about it, and I decided my loyalty shouldn't be to Mr. Yeager, it should be to the corporation. It paid my salary. So I told Mr. Aiken."

"What did he say?"

"He thanked me for telling him."

"What did he do?"

"I don't know. I don't know if he did anything."

"Did he speak to Mr. Yeager about it?"

"I don't know."

"Pfui. Certainly you know. If he had, Mr. Yeager would have known you told him. Did you remark any change in Mr. Yeager's attitude to you?"

"No."

"Did he continue to ask you to go there to take dictation?"

"Yes."

"How many times in the two months since you told Mr. Aiken?"

"Twice."

Wolfe shut his eyes and rubbed the bridge of his nose with a fingertip. Ten seconds. His eyes opened. "When did Mr. Aiken ask you to go there this evening?"

"This afternoon at the office. He asked if I still had the keys, and I said yes. He asked if I had ever told anyone else about that place, and I said no. He said it would be a great favor to the corporation if I would go there and make sure that—what I told you."

"Have you any reason to suppose that Mr. Aiken has ever been there?"

Her eyes widened. "Of course not."

He shook his head. "No, Miss McGee. No assumption is of course in an unsolved problem. I may if I choose assume that you have been entirely candid with me, but I may not—"

The doorbell rang. I got up and went, and there on the stoop was the president. The stoop light is at an angle on someone facing the door, from the side, so features aren't distinct, but the gray homburg and the fit of the gray topcoat were enough. I went and opened the door and asked, "Mr. Aiken? Come in."

He stayed put. "Am I expected?"

"Yes, sir. Miss McGee is with Mr. Wolfe."

He crossed the sill, and I helped him off with his coat. With his hat off, I recognized him; he had been seated near Thomas G. Yeager in the picture I had seen in Lon Cohen's office of the banquet of the National Plastics Association. His face was well formed and well kept, and though his hair was mostly gray, he still had it. Every inch a president. He had paid at least eight times as much for his suit as the phony Yeager had paid for his. When I convoyed him to the office he stopped four steps in and said, "Good evening, Miss McGee," then turned to Wolfe and said, "Good evening, sir. I'm Benedict Aiken."

She was on her feet. I thought she had risen to show respect, but Wolfe spoke to Aiken. "I have told Miss McGee that I'll speak with you privately first. If you please, madam? The door, Archie."

"Just a minute." Aiken wasn't belligerent, just firm. "I'd like to speak with Miss McGee myself."

"No doubt." Wolfe upturned a palm. "Mr. Aiken. What Miss McGee told you on the phone was correct except for one detail, that she was attacked. I stationed a man in that room on the chance that someone would come there. Miss McGee came, and she—"

"Why are you interested in that room?"

"Because it belonged to Thomas G. Yeager and was used by him. The man didn't attack Miss McGee; she attacked him. In explaining to me why she went there she mentioned you, and I would like an explanation from you so I can compare it with hers. She may be present if you prefer, but not if she tries to interrupt. If she does, Mr. Goodwin will stop her."

Aiken looked at me, sizing me up. He went to the red leather chair and sat, in no hurry, making himself comfortable with his elbows on the arms. His eyes went to Wolfe. "Why do you think that room belonged to Thomas G. Yeager?"

"I don't think, I know."

"Why are you concerned? Whom are you acting for?"

"Myself. I have no engagement. I am in possession of a fact about a man who was murdered that is not commonly known. I am not legally obliged to communicate it to the police, and I am exploring the possibility of using it to my profit—not by concealing it, but by exploiting it. Like doctors, lawyers, plumbers, and many others, I get my income from the necessities, the tribulations, and the misfortunes of my fellow beings. You are under no compulsion to tell me why *you* are concerned, but I am willing to listen. I didn't get you here."

Aiken was smiling, not with amusement. "I can't complain," he said, "since you have the handle. I didn't expect you to tell me who has hired you, but

it's hard to believe that no one has. How did you
find out about that room?"

Wolfe shook his head. "I owe you no light, sir.
But I have not been hired. If I had a client I would
say so, of course without naming him."

"How are you going to use the fact you possess
about that room?"

"I don't know. That will be determined by
events. My man is still there."

"When you speak of using it to your profit, of
course you mean get paid by somebody."

"Certainly."

"All right." Aiken shifted in the chair. "You want
to compare my explanation with Miss McGee's. Of
course you know that Yeager was the executive
vice-president of my corporation, Continental Plastic Products. Miss McGee was his secretary. Some
two months ago she came to me and told me about
that room, that Yeager had had her go there several
times in the evening to work with him on various
matters. She had no complaint of his conduct, but
she thought I should know about that room and
what it indicated of Yeager's character and habits.
From her description of the room I thought she was
fully justified. Obviously it was a difficult problem.
I asked her to mention it to no one, and not to refuse
to go there again; I would have to take time to
consider how to deal with it."

"Did you mention it to him?"

"No. I don't know how much you know of the
administrative complexities of a large corporation,
but the main question was whether the best procedure would be to discuss it with him first or take it
up with my board of directors. I still hadn't decided
yesterday when the news came that he was dead,

that his body had been found in a hole in the street in front of that house. Naturally that was a shock, that he had been murdered, that was—well, very unpleasant—but it would be worse than unpleasant, it would be disastrous, if the existence of that room became known. Since his body had been found in front of that house, it would be assumed that someone involved in his activities in that room had killed him, and the investigation, the publicity, the inevitable scandal would be terrible. I was going to call an emergency meeting of my board, but decided instead to consult three of my directors in confidence. It was possible that Yeager had kept the existence of that room so secret that his connection with it would not become known. I suggested asking Miss McGee to go there and get any articles that might identify Yeager, and the suggestion was approved. And your man was there." His head turned. "Exactly what happened, Miss McGee?"

"When I got out of the elevator, there he was," she said. "I guess I lost my head. I supposed he was a detective, a police detective. I tried to get back in the elevator, and he grabbed me, and I tried to get loose but couldn't. He folded a bed cover around me and strapped it tight, and made a phone call, and after a while this man came, Archie Goodwin. He found out who I was from things in my bag and told me they were working for Nero Wolfe and they knew it was Mr. Yeager's room, and since they knew that I thought I had better come here when he asked me to. He wouldn't let me phone until I got here. I'm sorry, Mr. Aiken, but what could I do?"

"Nothing." Aiken went back to Wolfe. "So that's why I am concerned. You won't deny that it's a legitimate concern?"

"No indeed. Legitimate and exigent. But also desperate; you can't possibly hope that Mr. Yeager's connection with that room will never be divulged."

"I don't hope. I act. Will you tell me how you learned about it?"

"No."

"I'll pay you for it. I'll pay well."

"I don't sell information, Mr. Aiken, I sell services."

"I'm buying them. You said you weren't engaged; you are now. I'm hiring you."

"To do what?"

"Whatever may be necessary to protect the reputation and interests of my corporation, Continental Plastic Products. I am acting for the corporation."

Wolfe shook his head. "I doubt if it would work. I couldn't undertake not to disclose Mr. Yeager's connection with that room; events might take charge. The alternative would be for me to take charge of events."

"How?"

"By guiding them. It would be futile for you to pay me not to reveal what I have learned about that room, even if I were ass enough to accept it; sooner or later the police will inevitably discover it, given time. The only feasible way to protect the reputation and interests of your corporation with any hope of success would be to stop the police investigation of the murder by reaching an acceptable solution of it without involving that room."

Aiken was frowning. "But that may be impossible."

"Also it may not be. It is highly probable that whoever killed him knew of that room and its character and function; but suppose, for instance, that it was an outraged husband or father or brother or paramour. That might conceivably be established without disclosing some of the particulars, including the place where the misconduct had occurred. It would be difficult, but it might be done. It would be pointless even to conjecture until more is known."

"And if it proved to be impossible?"

Wolfe's shoulders went up an eighth of an inch and down. "You will have wasted your money. My self-esteem is not up to tackling the impossible. I remark that you are coerced not by me but by the situation. You are threatened not by me but by my possession of a fact. So you want to hire me, and I am willing to be hired, but I will perform only those services that are proper to my calling and my probity. I can't exclude any possibility, even that you killed Yeager yourself."

Aiken smiled, again not with amusement. "I can."

"Naturally." Wolfe turned. "Archie, the typewriter. Two carbons."

I whirled my chair, pulled the machine around, arranged the paper with carbons, and inserted them. "Yes, sir."

"Single-spaced, wide margins. The date. On behalf of my corporation, Continental Plastic Products, I hereby engage Nero Wolfe to investigate the circumstances of the death of Thomas G. Yeager. It is understood that Wolfe will make every effort to protect the reputation and interests of the corporation, comma, and will disclose no facts or information that will harm the corporation's repute or prestige, comma, unless he is compelled to do so by his legal obligation as a citizen and a licensed private detective, semicolon; and if he fails to observe this provision he is to receive no pay for his services or reimbursement for his expenses. The purpose of this engagement of Nero Wolfe is to prevent, comma, as far as possible, comma, any damage to the corporation as a result of the special circumstances of Yeager's death. Below a space for signature put 'President, Continental Plastic Products.'"

I had typed it as he spoke. After taking it out and running over it, I handed the original to Aiken and the carbons to Wolfe. Aiken read it twice and looked up. "Your fee isn't specified."

"No, sir. It can't be. It will depend on what and how much I do."

"Who decides if you have faithfully observed the provision?"

"Reason and good faith, applied jointly. If that failed, it would be decided by a court, but that contingency is remote."

Aiken glanced over it again, put it on the stand at his elbow, took a pen from his pocket, and signed it. I took it and gave it to Wolfe and handed one of the carbons to Aiken. He folded it and stuck it in his pocket, and spoke.

"How and when did you learn about that room?"

Wolfe shook his head. "I don't start a difficult job by babbling, even to you." He glanced at the wall clock, pushed his chair back, and arose. "It's past midnight. I'll report to you, of course, but when and what is solely in my discretion."

"That's absurd. You're working for me."

"Yes, sir. But the only test of my performance is its result. It may be that the less you know of its particulars the better." He picked up the signed original. "Do you want this back?"

"No. I want to know how you're going to proceed."

"I don't know myself."

"You know this. Did one of my directors tell you about that room?"

"No."

"Did Mrs. Yeager tell you?"

"No."

"Then who did?"

Wolfe glared at him. "Confound it, sir, shall I drop this thing in the wastebasket? Do you want this job done or not?"

"It's not what I want, it's what I'm stuck with. You have the handle." He got up. "Come, Miss McGee."

Chapter 8

At half past ten Wednesday morning I stood by the big globe in the office, twirling it, trying to find a good spot to spend my vacation in the fall. Having spent a couple of hours trying to decide what I would tell me to do if I were Wolfe, and coming to the conclusion that the most sensible would be to go out and sweep the sidewalk, it had seemed advisable to put my mind on something else for a while. When Wolfe has instructions for me in the morning he sends word by Fritz that I am to come up to his room. That morning there had been no word, and at a quarter to nine I had buzzed him on the house phone. Getting nothing but a prolonged growl, I had started to make a list of the things he might have put on my program for the day and came up with that one item: sweeping the sidewalk.

I had done fine, no question about that. I had set out at nine o'clock Tuesday morning to dig up a client, and by midnight, in only fifteen hours, we had a beaut, not only the president of a big corporation but the corporation itself. To collect a five-figure fee all we had to do was earn it. So first we . . .

We what? Our big advantage was that we knew Yeager had been killed in that room, and probably no one else knew it but the Perez family and the murderer. We also knew that Yeager had expected female company Sunday evening, since he had ordered caviar and pheasant for midnight delivery. But granting that she had come, it didn't have to be that she had killed him; she might have found him dead on arrival. Taking it from that angle, the way to start would be to get a complete list of the women who had keys. That might be done in a year or so, and the next step would be to find out which one had— Nuts.

Of the three angles to a murder problem— means, opportunity, and motive—you pick the one that seems most likely to open a crack. I crossed off opportunity. Everyone who had keys had opportunity. Then means—namely, a gun capable of sending a bullet through a skull. It had not been found, so the way to go about it was to get a complete list of the people who had keys and also had access to a gun, and then— I crossed off means. Then motive. Having no personal experience of the methods and procedures in a bower of carnality, I wasn't qualified as an expert, but surely they might have aroused strong feelings in any or all of Yeager's guests. Say there had been ten different guests in the last couple of years. Allow them three apiece of husbands, brothers, fathers, and what Wolfe called paramours, and that made forty likely prospects with first-rate motives. I crossed off motive.

With means, opportunity, and motive hopeless, all you can do is go fishing. Catch somebody in a lie.

Find two pieces that are supposed to fit but don't. Find someone who saw or heard something—for example, someone in that house or that block who had noticed people entering or leaving the basement entrance of Number 156 who didn't appear to belong to the neighborhood. That program might get results if you had four or five good operatives and didn't care how long it took. But since Homicide might uncover a lead to that house any minute, and if they did they would find Fred Durkin there, and the fur would fly, and we would no longer have a client because what he wanted to buy couldn't be had, it wouldn't do. We needed either a genius or a lucky break.

Of course we had a genius, Nero Wolfe, but apparently he hadn't turned his switch on. When he came down from the plant rooms at eleven o'clock he put the day's orchid selection, Calanthe veitchi sandhurstiana, in the vase on his desk, circled to his chair and sat, glanced at his desk calendar, and looked through the morning crop of mail, which was mostly circulars and requests for contributions. He looked at me.

"What's this note on my calendar? Fourteen million, six hundred eighty-two thousand, two hundred thirty-five dollars and fifty-seven cents."

"Yes, sir. I got it from the bank. That's the cash reserve of Continental Plastic Products as shown on their statement dated January thirty-first. I thought you might like to know, and I had nothing else to do. I like to be busy at something."

"Pfui."

"Yes, sir. I agree."

"Have you considered the situation?"

"I have. It's a hell of a note. Yesterday, temporarily, we had too many clients. Two. Today we have one, and it's still too many because we can't possibly fill his order. If you're going to ask me for suggestions, don't bother. The only contribution I can make is worthless."

"What is it?"

"Julia McGee is a liar. You've heard that room described, but you haven't seen it. The man that fixed that room up, namely Yeager, did not have his secretary come there to take dictation. Any odds you want. Not even if she was a lump—he might have wanted to try an experiment—and she isn't. She has some very good points and possibilities, speaking as a satyr. So she lies, but that gets us nowhere. However she spent her evenings with him there, she could have done what she did do, squeal on him, either because the pictures bored her or because she wanted to get solid with the president. As far as the murder is concerned, it's a point in her favor. Having squealed on him, why should she shoot him? Do you want to ask her?"

"No." He took in air, all his barrel would hold, and let it out again. "I was a witling to take the job. All we can do is flounder around in the slush. As evidence of our extremity, it may be that we should find the man who got us into this pickle, despite our conclusion that he didn't know Yeager was dead. How long would it take you?"

"Something between a day and a year."

He made a face. "Or we could try a coup. We confront Mr. and Mrs. Perez with our conviction that they killed Yeager because he had defiled their daughter. We tell them that if the police learn of the room and Yeager's use of it they are probably doomed, as they are. Certainly they can't hope to

stay there indefinitely. We offer them a large sum,
twenty thousand, fifty thousand—no matter, it will
come from that cash reserve—to go to some far
corner of the earth, provided they will sign a
confession that they killed Yeager because their
daughter told them that he had made improper
advances to her. They need not admit that the
advances were successful; it can even be implied
that they were never made, that their daughter had
invented them. The confession will be left with us,
and we'll get it to the police anonymously after they
are safely out of reach. It will not mention that
room. Of course the police will find it, but there will
be nothing in it to connect it with Yeager. They will
assume that it was his, but they can't establish it,
and they do not publish assumptions that besmirch
a prominent citizen."

"Wonderful," I said with enthusiasm. "It only
has two minor flaws. First, since Yeager owned the
house, it will be an item in his estate. Second, they
didn't kill him. But what the hell, hanging a murder
on—"

"That's your opinion."

"With damn good legs under it. I'll concede that
you're being gallant, making Maria an inventor
instead of a floozy, but it would be even better—"

I was interrupted by the doorbell. Going to the
hall, I saw on the stoop what I have in mind, more
or less, when I apply the word "lump" to a female.
Not a hag, not a fright, just a woman, this one
middle-aged or more, who would have to be completely retooled and reassembled before she could
be used for show purposes. With her you would
have some spare parts left when you finished, for
instance the extra chin. Her well-made dark suit

and her platinum mink stole were no real help. I
went and opened the door and told her good morning.

"Nero Wolfe?" she asked.

I nodded. "His house."

"I want to see him. I'm Ellen Yeager. Mrs.
Thomas G. Yeager."

When a caller comes without an appointment, I
am supposed to leave him on the stoop until I
consult Wolfe, and I do, but this was a crisis. Not
only were we up a stump; there was even a chance
that Wolfe would be pigheaded enough to try that
cockeyed stunt with the Perez family if he wasn't
sidetracked. So I invited her to enter, led her to the
office and on in, and said, "Mr. Wolfe, Mrs. Yeager.
Mrs. Thomas G. Yeager."

He glared at me. "I wasn't informed that I had
an appointment."

"No, sir. You didn't."

"I didn't stop to phone," Ellen Yeager said. "It's
urgent." She went to the red leather chair and took
it as if she owned it, put her bag on the stand, and
aimed sharp little eyes at Wolfe. "I want to hire you
to do something." She reached for the bag, opened
it, and took out a checkfold. "How much do you
want as a retainer?"

Client number four, not counting the phony
Yeager. When I go scouting for clients I get results.
She was going on. "My husband was murdered, you
know about that. I want you to find out who killed
him and exactly what happened, and then *I* will
decide what to do about it. He was a sick man, he
was oversexed, I know all about that. I've kept still
about it for years, but I'm not going to let it keep
me from—"

Wolfe cut in. "Shut up," he commanded.

She stopped, astonished.

"I'm blunt," he said, "because I must be. I can't let you rattle off confidential information under the illusion that you are hiring me. You aren't and you can't. I'm already engaged to investigate the murder of your husband."

"You are not," she declared.

"Indeed?"

"No. You're engaged to keep it from being investigated, to keep it from coming out, to protect that corporation, Continental Plastic Products. One of the directors has told me all about it. There was a meeting of the board this morning, and Benedict Aiken told them what he had done and they approved it. They don't care if the murderer of my husband is caught or not. They don't want him caught. All they care about is the corporation. I'll own a block of stock now, but that doesn't matter. They can't keep me from telling the District Attorney about that room if I decide to."

"What room?"

"You know perfectly well what room. In that house on Eighty-second Street where Julia McGee went last night and you got her and brought her here. Benedict Aiken told the board about it, and one of them told me." Her head jerked to me. "Are you Archie Goodwin? I want to see that room. When will you take me there?" She jerked back to Wolfe. That's a bad habit, asking a question and not waiting for an answer, but it's not always bad for the askee. She opened the checkfold. "How much do you want as a retainer?"

She was impetuous, no question about that, but she was no fool, and she didn't waste words. She didn't bother to spell it out: and if Wolfe tried to do what she thought he had been hired to do, clamp a lid on it, she could queer it with a phone call to the DA's office, and therefore he had to switch to her.

He leaned back and clasped his fingers at the center of his frontal mound. "Madam, you have been misinformed. Archie, that paper Mr. Aiken signed. Let her read it."

I went and got it from the cabinet and took it to her. To read it she got glasses from her bag. She took the glasses off. "It's what I said, isn't it?"

"No. Read it again. Archie, the typewriter. Two carbons."

I sat, pulled the machine around, arranged the paper with carbons, and inserted them. "Yes, sir."

"Single-spaced, wide margins. The date. I, comma, Mrs. Thomas G. Yeager, comma, hereby engage Nero Wolfe to investigate the circumstances of the death of my late husband. The purpose of this engagement is to make sure that my husband's murderer is identified and exposed, comma, and Wolfe is to make every effort to achieve that purpose. If in doing so a conflict arises between his obligation under this engagement and his obligation under his existing engagement with Continental Plastic Products it is understood that he will terminate his engagemeent with Continental Plastic Products and will adhere to this engagement with me. It is also understood that I will do nothing to interfere with Wolfe's obligation to Continental Plastic Products without giving him notice in advance."

He turned to her. "No retainer is necessary; I have none from Mr. Aiken. Whether I bill you or not, and for what amount, will depend. I wouldn't expect a substantial payment from two separate clients for the same services. And I would expect none at all from you if, for instance, I found that you killed your husband yourself."

"You wouldn't get any. There was a time when I felt like killing him, but that was long ago when the children were young." She took the original from me and put on her glasses to read it. "This isn't right. When you find out who killed him you tell me and *I* decide what to do."

"Nonsense. The People of the State of New York will decide what to do. In the process of identifying him to my satisfaction and yours I will inevitably get evidence, and I can't suppress it. Archie, give her a pen."

"I'm not going to sign it. I promised my husband I would never sign anything without showing it to him."

A corner of Wolfe's mouth went up—his version of a smile. He was always pleased to get support for his theory that no woman was capable of what he called rational sequence. "Then," he asked, "shall I rewrite it, for me to sign? Committing me to my part of the arrangement?"

"No." She handed me the papers, the one Aiken had signed and the one she hadn't. "It doesn't do any good to sign things. What counts is what you do, not what you sign. How much do you want as a retainer?"

He had just said he didn't want one. Now he said. "One dollar."

Apparently that struck her as about right. She opened her bag, put the checkfold in it, took out a purse, got a dollar bill from it, and left the chair to hand it to Wolfe. She turned to me. "Now I want to see that room."

"Not now," Wolfe said with emphasis. "Now I have some questions. Be seated."

"What kind of questions?"

"I need information, all I can get, and it will take some time. Please sit down."

"What kind of questions?"

"Many kinds. You said that you have known for years that your husband was oversexed, that he was sick, so it may be presumed that you took the trouble to inform yourself as well as you could of his efforts to allay his ailment. I want names, dates, addresses, events, particulars."

"You won't get them from me." She adjusted her stole. "I quit bothering about it long ago. Once when the children were young I asked my doctor about it, if something could be done, perhaps some kind of an operation, but the way he explained it I knew my husband wouldn't do that, and there was nothing else I could do, so what was the use? I have a friend whose husband is an alcoholic, and she has a worse—"

The doorbell rang. Dropping the papers in a drawer and stepping to the hall, I did not see another prospective client on the stoop. Inspector Cramer of Homicide West has been various things—a foe, a menace, a neutral, once or twice an ally, but never a client; and his appearance through the one-way glass, the set of his burly shoulders and the expression on his big round red face, made it plain that he hadn't come to ante a retainer. I went and slipped the chain bolt on, opened the door the two inches it permitted, and spoke through the crack.

"Greetings. I don't open up because Mr. Wolfe has company. Will I do?"

"No. I know he has company. Mrs. Thomas G. Yeager has been here nearly half an hour. Open the door."

"Make yourself at home. I'll see." I shut the door, went to the office, and told Wolfe, "The tailor. He says his man brought the suit nearly half an hour ago, and he wants to discuss it."

He tightened his lips and scowled, at me, then at her, and back at me. Whenever an officer of the law appears on the stoop and wants in, his first impulse is to tell me to tell him he's busy and can't be disturbed, and all the better if it's Inspector Cramer. But the situation was already ticklish enough. If the cops had found a trail to that house and had followed it and found Fred Durkin there, the going would be fairly tough, and making Cramer pry his way in with a warrant would only make it tougher. Also there was Mrs. Yeager. Since Cramer knew she had been here nearly half an hour, obviously they had a tail on her, and it wouldn't hurt to know why. Wolfe turned to her.

"Inspector Cramer of the police is at the door, and he knows you're here."

"He does not." She was positive. "How could he?"

"Ask him. But it may be assumed that you were followed. You are under surveillance."

"They wouldn't dare! *Me?* I don't believe it! If they—"

The doorbell rang. Wolfe turned to me. "All right, Archie."

Chapter 9

At the meeting of those two, Wolfe and Cramer, naturally I am not an impartial observer. Not only am I committed and involved; there is also the basic fact that cops and private detectives are enemies and always will be. Back of the New York cop are the power and authority of eight million people; back of the private detective is nothing but the right to life, liberty, and the pursuit of happiness, and while that's a fine thing to have it doesn't win arguments. But though I am not impartial I'm an observer, and one of the privileges of my job is to be present when Cramer walks into the office and aims his sharp gray eyes at Wolfe, and Wolfe, his head cocked a little to the side, meets them. Who will land the first blow, and will it be a jab, a hook, or a swing?

On this occasion I got cheated. That first quick impact didn't take place because Mrs. Yeager didn't let it. As Cramer crossed the sill into the office she was there confronting him, demanding, "Am I being followed around?"

Cramer looked down at her. He was polite. "Good morning, Mrs. Yeager. I hope you haven't been annoyed. When there's a murderer loose we don't like to take chances. For your protection we thought it advisable—"

"I don't need any protection and I don't want any!" With her head tilted back the crease between her chins wasn't so deep. "Did you follow me here?"

"I didn't. A man did. We—"

"Where is he? I want to see him. Bring him in here. I'm telling you and I'm going to tell him, I will *not* be followed around. Protect me?" She snorted. "You didn't protect my husband. He gets shot on the street and put in a hole and you didn't even find him. A boy had to find him. Where's this man?"

"He was merely obeying orders." Cramer's tone sharpened a little. "And he followed you here, and maybe you *do* need protection. There are things to be protected from besides personal violence, like making mistakes. Maybe coming here was one. If you came to tell Nero Wolfe something you haven't told us, something about your husband, something that is or may be connected with his death, it *was* a mistake. So I want to know what you've said to him and what he said to you. All of it. You've been here nearly half an hour."

For half a second I thought she was going to spill it, and she did too. My guess would be that what popped into her mind was the notion that the simplest and quickest way to see that room on 82nd Street would be to tell Cramer abut it, and she might actually have acted on it if Wolfe's voice hadn't come at her from behind.

"I'll return your retainer if you want it, madam."

"Oh," she said. She didn't turn. "I hired him to do something," she told Cramer.

"To do what?"

"To find out who killed my husband. You didn't even find his body, and now all you do is follow me around, and this stuff about protecting me when there's nothing to protect me from. If I had anything to tell anybody I'd tell him, not you." She took a step. "Get out of the way; I'm going to see that man."

"You're making a mistake, Mrs. Yeager. I want to know what you said to Wolfe."

"Ask him." Seeing that Cramer wasn't going to move, she circled around him, headed for the hall. I followed her out and to the front. As I reached for the knob she came close, stretched her neck to get her mouth near my ear, and whispered, "When will you take me to see that room?" I whispered back, "As soon as I get a chance." I would have liked to stay at the door to see how she went about finding her tail, but if Cramer was going to blurt at Wolfe, "When did you take over that room on Eighty-second Street?" I wanted to be present, so I closed the door and went back to the office.

Cramer wasn't blurting. He was in the red leather chair, the front half of it, with his feet planted flat. Wolfe was saying, ". . . and that is moot. I'm not obliged to account to you for my acceptance of a retainer unless you charge interference with the performance of your official duty, and can support the charge."

"I wouldn't be here," Cramer said, "if I couldn't support it. It wasn't just the report that Mrs. Yeager was here that brought me. That would be enough, finding that you were sticking your nose into a murder investigation, but that's not all. I'm offering you a chance to cooperate by asking you a straight question: What information have you got about Yeager that might help to identify the person that killed him?"

So he knew about the room, and we were up a tree. I went to my desk and sat. It would be hard going, and probably the best thing for Wolfe to do would be to empty the bag and forget the clients.

He didn't. He hung on. He shook his head. "You know better than that. Take a hypothesis. Suppose, for instance, that I have been informed in confidence that a certain person owed Yeager a large sum of money and Yeager was pressing for payment. That *might* help to identify the murderer, but I am not obliged to pass the information on to you unless I am confronted with evidence that it *would* help. Your question is straight enough, but it's impertinent, and you know it."

"You admit you have information."

"I admit nothing. If I do have information the responsibility of deciding whether I am justified in withholding it is mine—and the risk."

"Risk my ass. With your goddam luck, and you talk about risk. I'll try a question that's more specific and maybe it won't be so impertinent. Why did Goodwin phone Lon Cohen at the *Gazette* at five o'clock Monday afternoon to ask for dope on Yeager, more than two hours before Yeager's body was found?"

I tried to keep my face straight, and apparently succeeded, since Cramer has good eyes with a lot of experience with faces, and if my relief had shown he would have spotted it. Inside I was grinning. They hadn't found the room; they had merely got a tip from some toad at the *Gazette* and had put the screws on.

Wolfe grunted. "That is indeed specific."

"Yeah. Now you be specific. I've seen you often enough horn in on a murder case, that's nothing new, but by God this is the first time you didn't even wait until the body was found. How did you know he was dead?"

"I didn't. Neither did Mr. Goodwin." Wolfe turned a hand over. "Mr. Cramer. I don't take every job that's offered to me. When I take one I do so to earn a fee, and sometimes it's necessary to take a calculated risk. I'm taking one now. It's true that someone, call him X, said something in this room Monday afternoon that caused Mr. Goodwin to phone Mr. Cohen for information about Thomas G. Yeager. But, first, nothing that X said indicated that he knew Yeager was dead, and it is our opinion that he did not know. Second, nothing that X said indicated that Yeager was in peril, that anyone intended to kill him or had any motive for killing him. Third, nothing that X said was the truth. We have discovered that every word he uttered was a lie. And since our conclusion that he didn't know Yeager was dead, and therefore he didn't kill him, is soundly based, I am justified in keeping his lies to myself, at least for the present. I have no information for you."

"Who is X?"

"I don't know."

"Nuts. Is it Mrs. Yeager?"

"No. I probably wouldn't name him even if I could, but I can't."

Cramer leaned forward. "Calculated risk, huh? Justified. You are like hell. I remember too many—"

The phone rang, and I swiveled and got it. "Nero Wolfe's offi—"

"I've got one, Archie."

My fingers tightened around the phone, and I pressed it closer to my ear. Fred again: "That you, Archie?"

"Certainly. I'm busy." If I told him to hold the wire and went to the kitchen, Cramer would step to my desk and pick it up.

"I said I've got another one. Another woman."

"I'm not sure that was sensible, Mr. Gerson. That might get you into serious trouble."

"Oh. Somebody there?"

"Certainly." Fred had good enough connections in his skull, but the service was a little slow. "I guess I'll have to, but I don't know how soon I can make it. Hold the wire a minute." I covered the transmitter and turned to Wolfe. "That damn fool Gerson has found his bonds and has got two of his staff locked in a room. He could get hooked for more damages than the bonds are worth. He wants me to come, and of course I ought to, but."

Wolfe grunted. "You'll have to. The man's a nincompoop. You can call Mr. Parker from there if necessary."

I uncovered the transmitter and told it, "All right, Mr. Gerson, I'm on my way. Keep them locked in till I get there." I hung up and went.

At the curb in front was Cramer's car. Trading waves with the driver, Jimmy Burke, I headed east. There was no reason to suppose that Cramer had a tail posted on me, but I wasn't taking the thinnest chance of leading a city employee to 82nd Street. Getting a taxi on Ninth Avenue, I told the driver I would give directions as we went along. We turned right on 34th Street, right again on Eleventh Avenue, right again on 56th Street, and left on Tenth

Avenue. By then I knew I was clear, but I kept an eye to the rear all the way to 82nd and Broadway. From there I walked.

The hole was being filled in. There was no uniform around, and no one in sight who might be representing Homicide West or the DA's bureau. Turning in at the basement entrance of 156, using Meg Duncan's key, and going down the hall, I had no feeling of eyes on me, but as I approached the end Cesar Perez appeared at the kitchen door.

"Oh, you," he said, and turned. "It's Mr. Goodwin."

His wife came from inside. "There's a woman up there," she said.

I nodded. "I came to meet her. Had you seen her before?"

"No." She looked at her husband. "Cesar, we must tell him."

"I don't know." Perez spread his hands. "You think better than I do, Felita. If you say so."

Her black eyes came at me. "If you're not an honest man, may the good God send us help. Come in here." She moved.

I didn't hesitate. Fred hadn't sounded on the phone as if he had any new scratches, and this pair might have something hot. I stepped into the kitchen. Mrs. Perez went to the table and picked up a card and handed it to me. "That man came this morning," she said.

It was the engraved card of a John Morton Seymour, with "Attorney at Law" in one corner and a midtown address in the other. "And?" I asked.

"He brought this." She picked up an envelope from the table and offered it. "Look at it."

It had been sealed and slit open. I took out a

paper with the regulation blue legal backing and
unfolded it. There were three typewritten sheets,
very neat and professional. I didn't have to read
every word to get the idea; it was a deed, signed by
Thomas G. Yeager and properly witnessed, dated
March 16, 1957, conveying certain property, namely
the house and ground at 156 West 82nd Street,
Borough of Manhattan, City of New York, to Cesar
and Felita Perez. First and most interesting question: how long had they known it existed?

"He brought that and gave it to us," she said.
"He said Mr. Yeager told him that if he died he must
give it to us within forty-eight hours after he died.
He said it was a little more than forty-eight hours
but he didn't think that would matter. He said he
would take care of it for us—formalities, he said—
without any charge. Now we have to tell you what
we were going to do. We were going away tonight.
We were going somewhere and not come back. But
now we argue, we fight. My husband and daughter
think we can stay, but I think we must go. For the
first time we fight more than just some words, so I
am telling you."

Cesar had an eye half closed. "What he say
yesterday," he said, "your Mr. Wolfe. He say when
they find out Mr. Yeager owned this house they
come here and then we have bad trouble, so we
decide to go tonight. But this man today, this Mr.
Seymour, he say Mr. Yeager did this paper like this
so nobody could know he owned this house and we
must not say he owned it. He say it is fixed so
nobody will know. So I say we can stay now. It is
our house now and we can take out the things we
don't want up there and it can be our room. If it's
too big we can put in walls. That kitchen and that

bathroom are beautiful. My wife thinks better than
I do nearly always, but this time I say I don't see
why. Why must we run away from our own house?"

"Well." I put the deed in the envelope and tossed
it on the table. "When Mr. Wolfe said yesterday
that you would be in trouble when they find out
that Yeager owned this house you knew they
wouldn't find out, and why didn't you say so?"

"You don't listen," Mrs. Perez said. "This Mr.
Seymour didn't come yesterday, he came this morning. You don't listen."

"Sure I do. But Yeager told you about that
paper long ago. You knew the house would be yours
if he died."

Her black eyes flashed. "If you listen do you call
us liars? When we say we were going away and this
Mr. Seymour comes with this paper, and now we
fight?"

I nodded. "I heard you. Have you got a Bible?"

"Of course."

"Bring it here."

She left the room, not to the hall, by another
door. In a moment she was back with a thick little
book bound in stiff brown leather. It didn't resemble
the Bibles I had seen, and I opened it for a look, but
it was in Spanish. Holding it, I asked them to put
their left hands on it and raise their right hands,
and they obliged. "Repeat this after me: I swear on
this Bible . . . that I didn't know . . . Mr. Yeager
was going to give us this house . . . and I had no
reason . . . to think he was going to . . . before
Mr. Seymour came this morning."

I put the Bible on the table. "Okay. If Mr.
Seymour says he can handle it so no one will know
Yeager owned it he probably can, but there are

quite a few people who already know it, including
me, so I advise you not to take anything from that
room, not a single thing, even if it's your property.
I also advise you to stay here. I'm not saying who
did the best thinking on that, but skipping out is the
worst thing you could possibly do. Yeager was
killed up there, and you moved the body. If you skip
it could even be that Mr. Wolfe will decide he has to
tell the police about you, and it wouldn't take them
long to find you, and swearing on a Bible wouldn't
help you then."

"They wouldn't find us," Mrs. Perez said.

"Don't kid yourself. Smarter people than you
have thought they could go where they couldn't be
found, and it can't be done. Forget it. I have to go
upstairs and see that woman. Please accept my
congratulations on having a house all your own.
May a cop never enter it."

I was going, but she spoke. "If we go away, we'll
tell you before we go."

"We're not going," Perez said. "We're citizens of
the United States of America."

"That's the spirit," I said, and went to the
elevator and pushed the button. It came, and I
entered and was lifted.

That bower of carnality grew on you. Emerging
from the elevator and seeing that all was serene,
that Fred hadn't had to use the coverlet again, I let
my eyes glance around. Unquestionably the place
had a definite appeal. It would have been an interesting and instructive experiment to move in and
see how long it would take to get used to it,
especially a couple of pictures across from the—

But I had work to do. Fred was in a yellow silk
chair, at ease, with a glass of champagne in his hand,

and on a couch facing him, also with a glass of
champagne, was a female who went with the sur-
roundings much better than either Meg Duncan or
Julia McGee, though of course they hadn't been
relaxed on a couch. This one was rather small, all
curves but not ostentatious, and the ones that
caught your eye and held it were the curves of her
lips—her wide, but not too wide, full mouth. As I
approached she extended a hand.

"I know you," she said. "I've seen you at the
Flamingo. I made a man mad once saying I wanted
to dance with you. When Fred said Archie Goodwin
was coming I had to sit down to keep from swoon-
ing. You dance like a dream."

I had taken the offered hand. Having shaken
hands with five different murderers on previous
occasions, I thought one more wouldn't hurt if it
turned out that way. "I'll file that," I told her. "If we
ever team up for a turn I'll try not to trample you.
Am I intruding? Are you and Fred old friends?"

"Oh no, I never saw him before. It just seems
silly to call a man Mister when you're drinking
champagne with him. I suggested the champagne."

"She put it in the freezer," Fred said, "and she
opened it, and why waste it? I don't like it much,
you know that."

"No apology needed. If she calls you Fred, what
do you call her?"

"I don't call her. She said to call her Dye. I was
just waiting for you."

On the couch, at arm's length from her, was a
leather bag shaped like a box. I was close enough so
that all I had to do to get it was bend and stretch an
arm. Her hand darted out, but too late, and I had it.

As I backed up a step and opened it, all she said was, "That's not nice, is it?"

"I'm only nice when I'm dancing." I went to the end of the couch and removed items one by one, putting them on the couch. There were only two things with names on them, an opened envelope addressed to Mrs. Austin Hough, 64 Eden Street, New York 14, and a driver's license, Dinah Hough, same address, thirty, five feet two inches, white, brown hair, hazel eyes. I put everything back in, closed the bag, and replaced it on the couch near her.

"I left the gun at home," she said, and took a sip of champagne.

"That was sensible. I only wanted to know how to spell Di. I may be able to save you a little trouble, Mrs. Hough. Nero Wolfe wants to see anyone who comes to this room and has keys to the door downstairs and the elevator—by the way, I left them in your bag—but if we went there now he'd be just starting lunch and you'd have to wait. We might as well discuss matters here while you finish the champagne."

"Will you have some? The bottle's in the refrigerator."

"No, thanks." I sat on the couch, four feet away, twisted around to face her. "I don't suppose the champagne's what you came here for. Is it?"

"No. I came to get my umbrella."

"Yellow with a red plastic handle?"

"No. Gray with a black handle."

"It's there in a drawer, but you'll have to manage without it for a while. If and when the police get interested in this place they won't like it if things have been taken away. How did it get here?"

"I need a refill." She was off of the couch and on her feet in one smooth movement. "Can't I bring you some?"

"No, thanks."

"You, Fred?"

"No, one's enough of this stuff."

She crossed to the kitchen door and on through. I asked Fred, "Did she try to buy you off or talk you off?"

He shook his head. "She didn't try anything. She gave me a look and saw I'm twice as big as she is, and she said, 'I don't know you, do I? What's your name?' She's a damn cool specimen if you ask me. Do you know what she asked me after we got talking? She asked me if I thought this would be a good place to have meetings of the Parent-Teachers Association. Believe me, if I was a woman and I had keys to this place and I came and found a stranger—"

Mrs. Hough had reappeared, with a full glass. She came and resumed her place on the couch without spilling a drop, lifted the glass, said, "Faith, hope, and charity," and took a sip. She adjusted her legs. "I left it here," she said. "Two weeks ago Friday, three weeks this coming Friday. It was raining. Tom Yeager had told me he knew a place that was different, worth seeing, he said, and he gave me keys and told me how to get in. When I came, this is what I found." She waved a hand. "You have to admit it's different. But there was no one here but him, and he had ideas I didn't like. He didn't actually assault me, say nothing but good of the dead, but he was pretty difficult, and I was glad to get away without my umbrella but with everything else."

She took a sip. "And when I read about his
death, about his body being found in a hole in the
street, this street, you can imagine. I wasn't worried about being suspected of having something to
do with his death, that wasn't it, but I knew how
clever they are at tracing things, and if the umbrella was traced to me, and this room described in
the papers—well . . ." She gestured. "My husband, my friends, everyone who knows me—and if
it got bad enough my husband might even lose his
job. But this place wasn't mentioned in the papers
yesterday, and when it wasn't mentioned again
today I thought they probably didn't know about it,
and I decided to come and see and perhaps I could
get my umbrella. So here I am."

She took a sip. "And you say I can't have it and
talk about going to see Nero Wolfe. It would be fun
to see Nero Wolfe, I wouldn't mind that, but I want
my umbrella, and I have an idea. You say it's here in
a drawer?"

"Right."

"Then *you* take it, and tonight take me to the
Flamingo and we'll dance. Not just a turn, we'll
dance till they close, and then you might feel like
letting me have the umbrella. That may sound
conceited, but I don't mean it that way, I just think
you *might*, and it won't hurt to find out, and anyhow
you'll have the umbrella."

"Yeah." The curve of her lips really caught the
eye. "And it won't be here. I appreciate the invitation, Mrs. Hough, but I'll be working tonight.
Speaking of working, why would your husband lose
his job? Does he work for Continental Plastic
Products?"

"No. He's an assistant professor at NYU. A wife

of a faculty member getting involved in a thing like this—even if I'm not really involved . . ."

There was a click in my skull. It wasn't a hunch; you never know where a hunch comes from; it was the word "professor" that flipped a switch. "What's he professor of?" I asked.

"English literature." She took a sip. "You're changing the subject. We can go to the Flamingo tomorrow night. You won't be losing anything except a few hours if you don't like me, because you'll have the umbrella." She looked at her wrist watch. "It's nearly half past one. Have you had lunch?"

"No."

"Take me to lunch and maybe you'll melt a little."

I was listening with only one ear. Teacher of literature. Measure your mind's height by the shade it casts, Robert Browning. I would have given ten to one, which would have been a sucker's bet, but a detective has as much right to look on the bright side as anyone else.

I stood up. "You're getting on my nerves, Mrs. Hough. It would be no strain at all to call you Di. I haven't seen anyone for quite a while that I would rather take to lunch or dance with, melting would be a pleasure, but I have to go. Nero Wolfe will still want to see you, but that can wait. Just one question: Where were you Sunday night from seven o'clock on?"

"No." Her eyes widened. "You *can't* mean that."

"Sorry, but I do. If you want to have another conference with yourself, I'll wait while you go to fill your glass again."

"You really mean it." She emptied the glass, taking her time. "I didn't go to the kitchen to have a conference with myself. Sunday night I was at home, at our apartment, with my husband. Seven o'clock on? We went to a restaurant in the Village a little after six for dinner, and got home after eight—around half past eight. My husband worked at some papers, and I read and watched television, and I went to bed around midnight, and stayed there, really I did. I seldom get up in the middle of the night and go and shoot a man and drop his body in a hole."

"It's a bad habit," I agreed. "Now Mr. Wolfe won't have to ask you that. I suppose you're in the phone book?" I turned to Fred. "Don't let her talk you out of the umbrella. How's the room service here? Okay?"

"No complaints. I'm beginning to feel at home. How much longer?"

"A day or a week or a year. You never had it softer."

"Hunh. You leaving her?"

"Yeah, she might as well finish the bottle. I've got an errand." As I made for the elevator Dinah Hough left the couch and headed for the kitchen. She was in there when the elevator came and I entered. Down below Mr. and Mrs. Perez were still in their kitchen, and I poked my head in and told them that their only hope of steering clear of trouble was to sit tight, and blew. At the corner of 82nd and Columbus was a drugstore where I could have treated my stomach to a glass of milk, but I didn't stop. I had a date with an assistant professor of English literature, though he didn't know it.

Chapter 10

It was 1:40 when I left that house. It was 6:10, four and a half hours later, when I said to Austin Hough, "You know damn well you can't. Come on."

During the four and a half hours I had accomplished a good deal. I had learned that in a large university a lot of people know where an assistant professor ought to be or might be, but no one knows where he is. I had avoided getting trampled in corridors twice, once by diving into an alcove and once by fighting my way along the wall. I had sat in an anteroom and read a magazine article entitled "Experiments in Secondary Education in Japan." I had sweated for fifteen minutes in a phone booth, reporting to Wolfe on the latest developments, including the acquisition of a house by Cesar and Felita Perez. I had taken time out to find a lunch counter on University Place and take in a corned-beef sandwich, edible, a piece of cherry pie, not bad, and two glasses of milk. I had been stopped in a hall by three coeds, one of them as pretty as a picture (no reference to the pictures on the top floor of the Perez house), who asked for my autograph. They probably took me for either Sir Laurence Olivier or Nelson Rockefeller, I'm not sure which.

And I never did find Austin Hough until I finally decided it was hopeless and went for a walk in the direction of 64 Eden Street. I didn't phone because his wife might answer, and it wouldn't have been tactful to ask if her husband was in. The thing was to get a look at him. So I went there and pushed the button in the vestibule marked Hough, opened the door when the click sounded, and entered, mounted two flights, walked down the hall to a door which opened as I arrived, and there he was.

He froze, staring. His mouth opened and closed. I said, not aggressively, just opening the conversation, "Other sins only speak; murder shrieks out."

"How in the name of God . . ." he said.

"How doesn't matter," I said. "We meet again, that's enough. Is your wife at home?"

"No. Why?"

"Why doesn't matter either if she's not here. There's nothing I'd enjoy more than chatting with you a while, but as you mentioned Monday, Mr. Wolfe comes down from the plant rooms at six o'clock, and he's in the office waiting for you. Come along."

He was deciding something. He decided it. "I don't know what you're talking about. I mentioned nothing to you Monday. I've never seen you before. Who are you?"

"I'm Thomas G. Yeager. His ghost. Don't be a sap. If you think it's just my word against yours, nuts. You can't get away with it. You know damn well you can't. Come on."

"We'll see if I can't. Take your foot away from the door. I'm shutting it."

There was no point in prolonging it. "Okay," I
said, "I'll answer the question you didn't finish. This
afternoon I had a talk with your wife. I got your
name and address from an envelope I took from her
bag."

"I don't believe it. That's a lie."

"Also in her bag was her driving license. Dinah
Hough, born April third, nineteen-thirty, white,
hair brown, eyes hazel. She likes champagne. She
tilts her head a little to the right when she—"

"Where did you see her?"

"Where doesn't matter either. That's all you'll
get from me. I told Mr. Wolfe I'd have you there at
six o'clock, and it's a quarter past, and if you
want—"

"Is my wife there?"

"No, not now. I'm telling you, Mr. Yeager—
excuse me, Mr. Hough—if you don't want all hell to
pop you'll take my hand and come along fast."

"Where's my wife?"

"Ask Mr. Wolfe."

He moved, and I sidestepped not to get bumped.
He pulled the door shut, tried it to make sure the
lock had caught, and headed for the stairs. I followed. On the way down I asked which direction
was the best bet for a taxi and he didn't reply. My
choice would have been Christopher Street, but he
turned right at the corner, toward Seventh Avenue,
and won the point. We had one in three minutes, at
the worst time of day. He had nothing to say en
route. There was a chance, one in ten, that Cramer
had a man staked to keep an eye on the old brownstone, but he wouldn't know Hough from Adam, and
going in the back way through the passage from
34th Street was complicated, so we rolled to the

curb in front. Mounting the stoop and finding the chain bolt was on, I had to ring for Fritz to let us in.

Wolfe was at his desk, scowling at a crossword puzzle in the *Observer*. He didn't look up as we entered. I put Hough in the red leather chair and went to mine, saying nothing. When a master brain is working on a major problem you don't butt in. In twenty seconds he muttered, "Confound it," slammed his pencil on the desk, swiveled, focused on the guest, and growled, "So Mr. Goodwin rooted you out. What have you to say for yourself?"

"Where's my wife?" Hough blurted. He had been holding it in.

"Wait a second," I put in. "I've told him I talked with his wife this afternoon and got his name and address from items in her bag. That's all."

"Where is she?" Hough demanded.

Wolfe regarded him. "Mr. Hough. When I learned Monday evening that a man named Thomas G. Yeager had been murdered, it would have been proper and natural for me to give the police a description of the man who had been here that afternoon impersonating him. For reasons of my own, I didn't. If I tell them about it now I'll give them not a description, but your name and address. Whether I do or not will depend on your explanation of that strange imposture. What is it?"

"I want to know where Goodwin saw my wife and why, and where she is. Until I know that, I'm explaining nothing."

Wolfe closed his eyes. In a moment he opened them. He nodded. "That's understandable. If your wife was a factor, you can't explain without involving her, and you won't do that unless she is already involved. Very well, she is. Monday afternoon, posing as Yeager, you told Mr. Goodwin that you expected to be followed to One-fifty-six West Eighty-second Street. When your wife entered a room in the house at that address at noon today, she found a man there who is in my employ. He notified Mr. Goodwin, and he went there and talked with her. She had keys to the house and the room. That's all I intend to tell you. Now your explanation."

I seldom feel sorry for people Wolfe has got in a corner. Usually they have asked for it one way or another, and anyhow if you can't stand the sight of a fish flopping on the gaff you shouldn't go fishing. But I had to move my eyes away from Austin Hough. His long bony face was so distorted he looked more like a gargoyle than a man. I moved my eyes away, and when I forced them back he had hunched forward and buried his face in his hands.

Wolfe spoke. "Your position is hopeless, Mr. Hough. You knew that address. You knew Yeager's unlisted telephone number. You knew that he frequented that address. You knew that your wife also went there. What did you hope to accomplish by coming here to send Mr. Goodwin on a pointless errand?"

Hough's head raised enough for his eyes to come to me. "Where is she, Goodwin?" It was an appeal, not a demand.

"I don't know. I left her in that room at that address at twenty minutes to two. She was drinking champagne but not enjoying it. The only other person there was the man in Mr. Wolfe's employ. He wasn't keeping her; she was free to go. I left because I wanted to have a look at you, but she didn't know that. I don't know when she left or where she went."

"You talked with her? She talked?"

"Right. Twenty minutes or so."

"What did she say?"

I sent a glance at Wolfe, but he didn't turn his head to meet it, so I was supposed to use my discretion and sagacity. I did so.

"She told me a lie, not a very good one. She said she had been there only once and hadn't stayed long. She had left her umbrella there and had gone today to get it. The part about the umbrella was okay; it was there in a drawer and still is. She invited me to take her to lunch. She invited me to take her to the Flamingo tonight and dance till they close."

"How do you know it was a lie, that she had been there only once?"

I shook my head. "You want too much for nothing. Just file it that I don't *think* she lied; I *know* she did. And I know you know it too."

"You do not."

"Oh, nuts. Go climb a rope."

Wolfe wiggled a finger at him. "Mr. Hough. We have humored you, but our indulgence isn't boundless. Your explanation."

"What if I don't give you one? What if I get up and walk out?"

"That would be a misfortune for both of us. Now that I know who you are I would be obliged to tell the police of your performance Monday afternoon, and I'd rather not, for reasons of my own. In that respect your interest runs with mine—and your wife's. Her umbrella is still there."

He was licked and he knew it. His face didn't go gargoyle again, but his mouth twisted and the skin around his eyes was squeezed in as if the light was too strong.

"Circumstances," he said. "Men are the sport of circumstances. Good God, as I sat in this chair talking to Goodwin, Yeager was dead, had been dead for hours. When I read it in the paper yesterday morning I knew how it would be if you found me, and I decided what to say; I was going to deny it, but now that won't do."

He nodded, slowly. "So. Circumstances. Of course my wife shouldn't have married me. It was a circumstance that she met me at a moment when she was—but I won't go into that. I'll try to keep to the point. I was a fool to think that I might still save our marriage, but I did. She wanted things that I couldn't supply, and she wanted to do things that I am not inclined to and not equipped for. She couldn't do them with me, so she did them without me."

"The point," Wolfe said.

"Yes. This is the first time I have ever said a word about my relations with my wife to anyone. About a year ago she suddenly had a watch that must have cost a thousand dollars or more. Then other things—jewelry, clothes, a fur coat. She had frequently spent evenings out without me, but it became more than evenings; occasionally she came home after dawn. You realize that now that I've started it's difficult to confine myself to the essentials."

"Do so if possible."

"I'll try. I descended to snooping. Curiosity creeps into the homes of the unfortunate under the names of duty or pity. When my wife—"

"Is that Pascal?"

"No, Nietzsche. When my wife went out in the

evening I followed her—not always, but when I could manage it. Mostly she went to a restaurant or the address of a friend I knew about, but twice she went to that address on Eighty-second Street and entered at the basement door. That was incomprehensible, in that kind of neighborhood, unless it was a dive of some sort—dope or God knows what. I went there one afternoon and pushed the button at the basement door, but learned nothing. I am not a practiced investigator like you. A man, I think a Puerto Rican, told me only that he had no vacant rooms."

He stopped to swallow. "I also snooped at home, and one day I found a phone number that my wife had scribbled on the back of an envelope. Chisholm five, three-two-three-two. I dialed it and learned that it was the residence of Thomas G. Yeager. It wasn't listed. I made inquiries and found out who he was, and I saw him, more by luck than design. Do you want to know how it happened?"

"No. You met him?"

"No, I saw him at a theater. That was two weeks ago. And three days later, Friday, a week ago last Friday, I followed her when she went out, and she went again, that was the third time, to that house on Eighty-second Street. I went and stood across the street, and very soon, not more than five minutes, Yeager came, walking. It was still daylight. He turned in, to the basement entrance, and entered. What would you have done?"

Wolfe grunted. "I wouldn't have been there."

Hough turned to me. "What would you have done, Goodwin?"

"That's irrelevant," I said. "I'm not you. You

might as well ask what I would do if I were a robin and saw a boy robbing my nest. What did you do?"

"I walked up and down the block until people began to notice me, and then went home. My wife came home at six o'clock. I didn't ask her where she had been; I hadn't asked her that for a year. But I decided I must do something. I considered various things, various plans, and rejected them. I finally settled on one Sunday evening. We had had dinner—"

"Which Sunday?"

"Last Sunday. Three days ago. We had had dinner at a restaurant and returned home. My wife was watching television, and I was in my room working, only I wasn't working. I was deciding what to do, and the next day I did it. I came here and saw Archie Goodwin. You know what I said to him."

"Yes. Do you think you've accounted for it?"

"I suppose not. It was like this: I knew that when Yeager didn't turn up Goodwin would find out why, either phone him—that was why I gave him the number—or go to the house. He would want to *see* Yeager, and he would tell him about me and what I had said. So Yeager would know that someone, someone he wouldn't identify from Goodwin's description, knew about his going to that house. He would know that Archie Goodwin and Nero Wolfe also knew about it. And he would tell my wife about it and describe me to her, and she would know I knew. That was the most important. I couldn't tell her, but I wanted her to know that I knew."

His eyes came to me and returned to Wolfe. "Another thing. I knew that Archie Goodwin wouldn't just dismiss it from his mind. He would wonder why I had mentioned that particular address, and he would wonder what secret connection there might be between Yeager and that house in that neighborhood, and when Archie Goodwin wonders about anything he finds out. All of this was in my mind, but the most important was that my wife would know that I knew."

His mouth worked, and he gripped the chair arms. "And that evening on the radio, the eleven-o'clock news, I learned that Yeager was dead, and yesterday morning in the paper I learned that he had died, had been murdered, Sunday night, and his body had been found in a hole in front of that house. Thank God my wife wasn't there Sunday night."

"You're sure of that?"

"Certainly I'm sure. We sleep in separate beds, but when she turns over I hear her. You realize—" He stopped.

"What?"

"Nothing. I was going to say you realize that I have told you things I wouldn't have thought I could possibly ever tell anybody, but you don't care about that. Perhaps I have blundered again, but I was trapped by circumstance. Is there any chance, any chance at all, that it will stay with you? I can't ask you for any consideration, I know that, after the way I imposed on Goodwin Monday afternoon. But if you could find it possible . . ."

Wolfe looked up at the clock. "It's my dinner-time. It doesn't please me to hurt a man needlessly, Mr. Hough, and your puerile imposition on Mr. Goodwin doesn't rankle. On the contrary; you gave him that address and he went there, and as a result we have a client." He pushed his chair back and rose. "What you have told us will be divulged only if it becomes requisite."

"Who is your client?"

When Wolfe said that was hardly his concern, he didn't try to insist. I permitted myself to feel sorry for him again as he left the chair. He was in a hell of a spot. He wanted to see his wife, he *had* to see her, but what was he going to say? Was he going to explain that he was responsible for her finding a reception committee when she went to get her umbrella? Was he going to admit—I turned that switch off. He had married her, I hadn't. When I went to the front to let him out, I stood on the stoop for a minute to see if there was someone around who was curious enough about him to follow him. There wasn't. I shut the door and went to join Wolfe in the dining room.

The two letters in the morning mail hadn't been answered, and when we returned to the office after dinner and had finished coffee we attended to them. One was from a Putnam County farmer asking how many starlings he wanted this year, and the other was from a woman in Nebraska saying that she would be in New York for a week late in June, with her husband and two children, and could they come and look at the orchids. The reply to the first was forty; Wolfe always invites two dinner guests for the starling pie. The reply to the second was no; she shouldn't have mentioned the children. When the answers had been typed and Wolfe had signed them, he sat and watched while I folded them and put them in the envelopes, and then spoke.

"Your exclusion of Mr. and Mrs. Perez is no longer valid. They knew they would get the house."

Of course I had known that was coming. I

swiveled. "It's a funny thing about the Bible. I haven't been to church for twenty years, and modern science has proved that heaven is two hundred degrees Fahrenheit hotter than hell, but if I was asked to put my hand on a Bible and swear to a lie, I'd dodge. I'd say I was a Hindu or a Buddhist— Zen, of course. And Mr. and Mrs. Perez undoubtedly go to mass once a week and probably oftener."

"Pfui. To get a house, perhaps not; but to save their skins?"

I nodded. "Thousands of murderers have lied under oath on the witness stand, but this was different. They still sort of think I'm their detective."

"You're incorrigibly mulish."

"Yes, sir. Same to you."

"Nor is that imbecile Hough excluded. I call him an imbecile, but what if he is in fact subtle, wily, and adroit? Knowing or suspecting that his wife was going to that address Sunday evening, he got her keys, went there himself, killed Yeager, and left. Monday something alarmed him, no matter what; perhaps he told his wife what he had done, or she guessed, and her attitude brought dismay. He decided he must take some action that would make it seem highly unlikely that he had been implicated, and he did. You and I concluded yesterday that the impostor had not known Yeager was dead—not an assumption, a conclusion. We now abandon it."

"It's not incredible," I conceded. "I see only three holes in it."

"I see four, but none of them is beyond patching. I'm not suggesting that we have advanced; indeed, we have taken a step backward. We had concluded that that man was eliminated, but he isn't. And now?"

We discussed it for two solid hours. By the time we went up to bed, toward midnight, it looked very much as if we had a case and a client, two clients, and we didn't hold one single card that we were in a position to play. Our big ace, that we knew about that room and that Yeager had been killed in it, was absolutely worthless. And the longer we kept it up our sleeve, the more ticklish it would be when the police found a trail to it, as they were bound to sooner or later. When Wolfe left for his elevator he was so sour that he didn't say good night. As I undressed I was actually weighing the chance, if we called Fred off, that the cops wouldn't pry it loose that we had been there. That was so ridiculous that I turned over three times before I got to sleep.

The phone rang.

I understand that some people, when the phone rings in the middle of the night, surface immediately and are almost awake by the time they get it to their ear. I don't. I am still way under. I couldn't possibly manage anything as complicated as "Nero Wolfe's residence, Archie Goodwin speaking." The best I can do is " 'Lo."

A woman said, "I want to talk to Mr. Archie Goodwin." I was still fighting my way up.

"This is Goodwin. Who is this?"

"I am Mrs. Cesar Perez. You must come. Come now. Our daughter Maria is dead. She was killed with a gun. Will you come now?"

I was out from under. "Where are you?" I reached for the switch of the bed light and glanced at the clock. Twenty-five to three.

"We are at home. They took us to look at her, and we are just come back. Will you come?"

"Is anybody there? Policemen?"

"No. One brought us home, but he is gone. Will you come?"

"Yes. Right away. As fast as I can make it. If you haven't already—"

She hung up.

I like to take my time dressing, but I am willing to make an exception when necessary. When my tie was tied and my jacket on, and my things were in my pockets, I tore a sheet from my notebook and wrote on it:

Maria Perez is dead, murdered, shot—not at home, I don't know where. Mrs. P. phoned at 2:35. I'm on my way to 82nd Street.

AG

Down one flight I went to the door of Wolfe's room and slipped the note through the crack at the bottom. Then on down, and out. At that time of night Eighth Avenue would be the best bet for a taxi, so I headed east.

Chapter 11

It was one minute after three when I used my key at the basement door at 156 and entered. Mrs. Perez was standing there. Saying nothing, she turned and walked down the hall, and I followed. Halfway along she turned into a room on the right, the door of which I had pushed open Tuesday evening when I felt an eye on me. It was a small room; a single bed, a chest of drawers, a little table with a mirror, and a couple of chairs didn't leave much space. Perez was on the chair by the table, and on the table was a glass and a bottle of rum. As I entered he slowly lifted his head to look at me. The eye that he half closed in emergencies was nearly shut.

He spoke. "My wife told you that day we sit down with friends. Are you a friend?"

"Don't mind him," she said. "He drinks rum, half a bottle. I tell him to." She sat on the bed. "I make him come to this room, our daughter's room, and I bring him rum. I sit on our daughter's bed. That chair is for you. We thank you for coming, but now we don't know why. You can't do anything, nobody can do anything, not even the good God Himself."

Perez picked up the glass, took a swallow, put the glass down, and said something in Spanish.

I sat on the chair. "The trouble with a time like this," I said, "is that there *is* something to do, and the quicker the better. You have no room in you right now for anything except that she's dead, but I have. I want to know who killed her, and you will too when the shock eases up a little. And in order—"

"You're crazy," Perez said. "I'll kill him."

"He's a man," she told me. I thought for a second she meant that a man had killed Maria and then realized that she meant her husband.

"We'll have to find him first," I said. "Do you know who killed her?"

"You're crazy," Perez said. "Of course not."

"They took you to look at her. Where? The morgue?"

"A big building," she said. "A big room with strong light. She was on a thing with a sheet on her. There was blood on her head but not on her face."

"Did they tell you who found her and where?"

"Yes. A man found her at a dock by the river."

"What time did she leave the house and where did she go and who with?"

"She left at eight o'clock to go to a movie with friends."

"Boys or girls?"

"Girls. Two girls came for her. We saw them. We know them. We went with a policeman to see one of them, and she said Maria went with them to the movie but she left about nine o'clock. She didn't know where she went."

"Have you any idea where she went?"

"No."

"Have you any idea who killed her or why?"

"No. They asked us all these questions."

"They'll ask a lot more. All right, this is how it stands. Either there is some connection between her death and Mr. Yeager's death or there isn't. If there isn't, it's up to the police and they'll probably nail him. Or her. If there is, the police can't even get started because they don't know this was Yeager's house—unless you've told them. Have you?"

"No," she said.

"You're crazy," he said. He took a swallow of rum.

"Then it's up to you. If you tell them about Yeager and that room, they may find out who killed Maria sooner than I would. Mr. Wolfe and I. If you don't tell them, we'll find him, but I don't know how long it will take us. I want to make it clear: If her death had nothing to do with Yeager, it won't hamper the police any not to know about him and that room, so it wouldn't help to tell them. That's that. So the question is, what do you want to do if it did have something to do with Yeager? Do you want to tell the police about him and the house, and probably be charged with killing Yeager? Or do you want to leave it to Mr. Wolfe and me?"

"If we had gone away last night," Mrs. Perez said. "She didn't want to. If I had been strong enough—"

"Don't say that," he commanded her. "Don't say that!"

"It's true, Cesar." She got up and went and poured rum in his glass, and returned to the bed. She looked at me. "She never had anything with Mr. Yeager. She never spoke to him. She never was in that room. She knew nothing about all that, about him and the people that came."

"I don't believe it," I declared. "It's conceivable that an intelligent girl her age wouldn't be curious about what was going on in the house she lived in, but I don't believe it. Where was she Sunday night when you took Yeager's body out and put it in the hole?"

"She was in her bed asleep. This bed I'm sitting on."

"You thought she was. She had good ears. She heard me enter the house Tuesday evening. When I came down the hall the door to this room was open a crack and she was in here in the dark, looking at me through the crack."

"You're crazy," Perez said.

"Maria wouldn't do that," she said.

"But she did. I opened the door and we spoke, just a few words. Why shouldn't she do it? A beautiful, intelligent girl, not interested in what was happening in her own house? That's absurd. The point is this: If you're not going to tell the police about Yeager, if you're going to leave it to Mr. Wolfe and me, I've got to find out what she knew, and what she did or said, that made someone want to kill her. Unless I can do that there's no hope of getting anywhere. Obviously I won't get it from you. Have the police done any searching here?"

"Yes. In this room. The first one that came."

"Did he take anything?"

"No. He said he didn't."

"I was here," Perez said. "He didn't."

"Then if you're leaving it to us that comes first. I'll see if I can find something, first this room and then the others. Two can do it faster than one, so

will you go up and tell that man to come—no.
Better not. He already knows too much for his own
good. What you two ought to do is go to bed, but I
suppose you won't. Go to the kitchen and eat
something. You don't want to be here while I'm
looking. I'll have to take the bed apart. I'll have to
go through all her things."

"It's no good," Mrs. Perez said. "I know everything she had. We don't want you to do that."

"Okay. Then Mr. Wolfe and I are out and the
police are in. It won't be me looking, it will be a
dozen of them, and they're very thorough, and you
won't be here. You'll be under arrest."

"That don't matter now," Perez said. "Maybe I
ought to be." He lifted the glass, and it nearly
slipped from his fingers.

Mrs. Perez rose, went to the head of the bed,
and pulled the coverlet back. "You'll see," she said.
"Nothing."

An hour and a half later I had to admit she was
right. I had inspected the mattress top and bottom,
emptied the drawers, removing the items one by
one, taken up the rug and examined every inch of
the floor, removed everything from the closet and
examined the walls with a flashlight, pulled the
chest of drawers out and inspected the back, flipped
through thirty books and a stack of magazines,
removed the backing of four framed pictures—the
complete routine. Nothing. I was much better ac-
quainted with Maria than I had been when she was
alive, but hadn't found the slightest hint that she
knew or cared anything about Yeager, his guests, or
the top floor.

Perez was no longer present. He had been in the
way when I wanted to take up the rug, and by that

time the rum had him nearly under. We had taken
him to the next room and put him on the bed.
Maria's bed was back in order, and her mother was
sitting on it. I was standing by the door, rubbing my
palms together, frowning around.

"I told you, nothing," she said.

"Yeah. I heard you." I went to the chest and
pulled out the bottom drawer.

"Not again," she said. "You are like my husband.
Too stubborn."

"I wasn't stubborn enough with these drawers."
I put it on the bed and began removing the contents. "I just looked at the bottoms underneath. I
should have turned them over and tried them."

I put the empty drawer upside down on the
floor, squatted, jiggled it up and down, and tried the
edges of the bottom with the screwdriver blade of
my knife. Saul Panzer had once found a valuable
painting under a false bottom that had been fitted
on the outside instead of the inside. This drawer
didn't have one. When I put it back on the bed Mrs.
Perez came and started replacing the contents, and
I went and got the next drawer.

That was it, and I darned near missed it again.
Finding nothing on the outside of the bottom, as I
put the drawer back on the bed I took another look
at the inside with the flashlight, and saw a tiny hole,
just a pinprick, near a corner. The drawer bottoms
were lined with a plastic material with a pattern,
pink with red flowers, and the hole was in the
center of one of the flowers. I got a safety pin from
the tray on the table and stuck the point in the hole
and pried, and the corner came up, but it was stiffer
than any plastic would have been. After lifting it
enough to get a finger under, I brought it on up and

had it. The plastic had been pasted to a piece of cardboard that precisely fitted the bottom of the drawer, and underneath was a collection of objects which had been carefully arranged so there would be no bulges. Not only had Maria been intelligent, she had also been neat-handed.

Mrs. Perez, at my elbow, said something in Spanish and moved a hand, but I blocked it. "I have a right," she said, "my daughter."

"Nobody has a right," I said. "She was hiding it from you, wasn't she? The only right was hers, and she's dead. You can watch, but keep your hands off." I carried the drawer to the table and sat in the chair Perez had vacated.

Here's the inventory of Maria's private cache:

1. Five full-page advertisements of Continental Plastic Products taken from magazines.

2. Four labels from champagne bottles, Dom Pérignon.

3. Three tear sheets from the financial pages of the *Times*, the stock-exchange price list of three different dates with a pencil mark at the Continental Plastic Products entries. The closing prices of CPP were 62½, 61⅝, and 66¾.

4. Two newspaper reproductions of photographs of Thomas G. Yeager.

5. A newspaper reproduction of a photograph of Thomas G. Yeager, Jr., and his bride, in their wedding togs.

6. A newspaper reproduction of a photograph of Mrs. Thomas G. Yeager, Sr., with three other women.

7. A full-page reproduction from a picture magazine of the photograph of the National Plastics Association banquet in the Churchill ballroom, of which I had seen a print in Lon

138   Rex Stout

Cohen's office Monday evening. The caption
gave the names of the others on the stage with
Yeager, including one of our clients, Benedict
Aiken.

8. Three reproductions of photographs of Meg
Duncan, two from magazines and one from a
newspaper.

9. Thirty-one pencil sketches of women's
heads, faces, some with hats and some without.
They were on 5-by-8 sheets of white paper, of
which there was a pad on Maria's table and two
pads in a drawer. In the bottom left-hand corner
of each sheet was a date. I am not an art expert,
but they looked pretty good. From a quick
run-through I guessed that there were not
thirty-one different subjects; there were second
and third tries of the same face, and maybe four
or five. The dates went back nearly two years,
and one of them was May 8, 1960. That was last
Sunday. I gave the drawing a good long look. I
had in my hand a promising candidate for a
people's exhibit in a murder trial. Not Meg
Duncan, and not Dinah Hough. It could be Julia
McGee. When I realized that I was deciding it
was Julia McGee I quit looking at it. One of the
brain's most efficient departments is the one
that turns possibilities into probabilities, and
probabilities into facts.

10. Nine five-dollar bills of various ages.

Mrs. Perez had moved the other chair beside me
and was on it. She had seen everything, but had
said nothing. I looked at my watch: twenty minutes
to six. I evened the edges of the tear sheets from
the *Times,* folded them double, and put the other
items inside the fold. The question of obstructing
justice by suppressing evidence of a crime was no
longer a question. My lawyer might maintain that I

had assumed that that stuff wasn't relevant to the murder of Yeager, but if he told a judge and jury that I had also assumed that it wasn't relevant to the murder of Maria Perez, he would have to concede that I was an idiot.

With the evidence in my hand, I stood up. "All this proves," I told Mrs. Perez, "is that Maria had the normal curiosity of an intelligent girl and she liked to draw pictures of faces. I'm taking it along, and Mr. Wolfe will look it over. I'll return the money to you some day, I hope soon. You've had a hard night and you've got a hard day ahead. If you have a dollar bill, please get it and give it to me. You're hiring Mr. Wolfe and me to investigate the murder of your daughter; that's why you're letting me take this stuff."

"You were right," she said.

"I've earned no medals yet. The dollar, please?"

"We can pay more. A hundred dollars. It doesn't matter."

"One will do for now."

She got up and went, and soon was back with a dollar bill in her hand. She gave it to me. "My husband is asleep," she said.

"Good. You ought to be too. We are now your detectives. A man will come sometime today, and he'll probably take you and your husband down to the District Attorney's office. They won't mention Yeager, and of course you won't. About Maria, just tell them the truth, what you've already told the policeman, about her going to the movie, and you don't know who killed her or why. Have you been getting breakfast for the man up above?"

"Yes."

"Don't bother this morning. He'll be leaving

pretty soon and he won't come back." I offered a hand, and she took it. "Tell your husband we're friends," I said, and went out to the elevator.

Emerging into the bower of carnality, I switched on the light. My mind was so occupied that the pictures might as well not have been there, and anyway there was a living picture: Fred Durkin on the eight-foot-square bed, his head on a yellow pillow, and a yellow sheet up to his chin. As the light went on he stirred and blinked, then stuck his hand under the pillow and jerked it out with a gun in it.

"At ease," I told him. "I could have plugged you before you touched it. We've got all we can use, and it's time to go. There's no rush; it'll be fine if you're out of here in half an hour. Don't stop down below to find Mrs. Perez and thank her; they're in trouble. Their daughter was murdered last night—not here, not in the house. Just blow."

He was on his feet. "What the hell is this, Archie? What am I in?"

"You're in three hundred bucks. I advise you to ask me no questions; I might answer them. Go home and tell your wife you've had a rough two days and nights and need a good rest."

"I want to know one thing. Am I going to get tagged?"

"Toss a coin. I hope not. We could be lucky."

"Would it help if I wipe up here? Ten minutes would be it."

"No. If they ever get this far they won't need fingerprints. Go home and stay put. I may be ringing you around noon. Don't take any of the pictures."

I entered the elevator.

Chapter 12

When Wolfe came down from the plant rooms at eleven o'clock I was at my desk with the noon edition, so-called, of the *Gazette*. There was a picture of Maria Perez, dead, on the front page. She didn't really rate it, since she had had absolutely no distinction but youth and beauty, but she got a break because nobody important had been killed or robbed or arrested that night.

It was wide open. The only facts they had, leaving off the tassels, were: a) the body had been found at 12:35 a.m. by a watchman making his rounds on a North River pier in the Forties; b) she had been dead not more than three hours and probably less; c) she had been shot in the back of the head with a .32; d) she had last been seen alive by the two girl friends who had gone to the movie with her, and who said she had got up and left a little before nine o'clock and hadn't come back; she had said nothing to them; they had supposed she was going to the rest room; and e) her father and mother refused to talk to reporters. There was no hint of any suspicion that there was any connection between her death and that of Thomas G. Yeager, whose body had been found three days earlier in a hole in the street she had lived on.

I had reported briefly to Wolfe after his breakfast in his room, just the essentials. Now, as he sat at his desk, I handed him the *Gazette*. He glanced at the picture, read the story, put the paper down, and leaned back.

"Verbatim," he said.

I gave him the crop, including, of course, my call on Fred. When I had finished I handed him the evidence I had got from Maria's drawer. "One item," I said, "might mislead you—labels from four champagne bottles. I do not and will not believe that Maria drank any of the champagne. She got the labels when her father or mother brought the bottles down to dispose of them."

"Who said so?"

"I say so."

He grunted and began his inspection. With that sort of thing he always takes his time. He looked at the back of each item as well as the front, even the advertisements, the five-dollar bills, and the tear sheets from the *Times*. Finishing with them, the labels, and the photographs, he handed them to me and tackled the drawings. After running through them, five seconds for some and up to a minute for others, he stood up and began laying them out on his desk in rows. They just about covered it. I stood and watched as he shifted them around into groups, each group being presumably different sketches of the same woman. Twice I disagreed and we discussed it. We ended up with three groups with four sketches each, five groups with three sketches each, one group with two, and two with only one.

Eleven different guests in two years, and it wasn't likely that Maria had got all of them. Yeager had been a very hospitable man.

I pointed to one of the four-sketch groups. "I can name her," I said. "Ten to one. I have danced with her. Her husband owns a chain of restaurants and is twice her age."

He glared at me. "You're being frivolous."

"No, sir. The name is Delancey."

"Pfui. Name that one." He pointed to the two-sketch group. "One dated April fifteenth and the other May eighth. Last Sunday."

"I was leaving it to you. You name it."

"She has been in this room."

"Yes, sir."

"Julia McGee."

"Yes, sir. I wasn't being frivolous. I wanted to see if you would spot her. If those are the dates Maria saw the subjects in the hall, not merely the dates she made these sketches, Julia McGee was there Sunday. Either she killed him or she found him dead. If he was on his feet when she arrived she wouldn't have left before midnight, because refreshments were expected—and of course she didn't go to take dictation. And if he was alive and she was there when the murderer came she would have got it too. So if she didn't kill him she found him dead. By the way, to clear up a detail, I have entered the dollar Mrs. Perez gave me in the cash book as a retainer. I took it because I thought she would be more likely to hold on if she had us hired, and I assumed they are now eliminated. They didn't kill their daughter. I am not crowing. I would rather have been wrong than be proved right by having Maria get it, even if she asked for it."

"That she asked for it is only conjecture."

"Yeah. But our theory is that she was killed by the person who killed Yeager or we haven't got a theory, and in that case Maria must have made the contact. Suppose it was Julia McGee. She couldn't have known there was an eye on her behind that crack as she went down the hall, or if she did she couldn't have known whose eye it was. If she felt or suspected it, as I did, and pushed the door open and found Maria there, she wouldn't have gone up and used the gun she had brought to shoot Yeager. So Maria must have made the contact yesterday, and she wouldn't do that just for the hell of it, just for the pleasure of saying, 'I saw you come in Sunday evening so I know you killed Mr. Yeager.' She wanted to make a deal. That she asked for it may be only a conjecture, but I don't make it because I like it. I would prefer to believe that she was as good inside as outside. Anyhow she didn't drink that champagne."

Wolfe said, "Mmmmh."

I pointed to one of the three-sketch groups. "That's Dinah. Mrs. Austin Hough. Maria knew how to get a likeness. She got Mrs. Delancey too."

"There is none of Meg Duncan."

"No. When she got photographs of her she didn't need a sketch."

He sat down. "Get Fred. How soon can he be here?"

"Twenty minutes."

"Get him."

I got at my phone and dialed, and Fred answered. I told him that if he could make it here in nineteen minutes two things would be waiting for him, $315 and instructions from Wolfe, and he said both would be welcome. I turned and told Wolfe, and he said, "Get Miss McGee. I'll speak to her."

That took a little longer. The trouble seemed to be, when I got the Continental Plastic Products switchboard, that Julia McGee had been Yeager's secretary, and now that he was no longer there the operator didn't know where Miss McGee was. I finally got her and signed to Wolfe, and he took his phone. I stayed on.

"Miss McGee? I must see you as soon as possible. At my office."

"Well—" She didn't sound enthusiastic. "I leave at five. Will six o'clock do?"

"No, it's urgent. As soon as you can get here."

"Can't you tell me on the phone—no, I suppose not. All right, I'll come."

"Now."

"Yes. I'll leave in a few minutes."

We hung up. Wolfe leaned back and closed his eyes. I gathered up the drawings and put them with the rest of Maria's collection. Getting a folder from the cabinet, I marked it YEAGER and put the collection in it, decided that the safe was the proper place for something that might some day be a people's exhibit, and took it there instead of the cabinet. When Wolfe's eyes opened I took him a check to sign, to Fred Durkin for three hundred fifteen & 00/100 dollars. We were now out about five Cs on the Yeager operation, and we had four clients and two bucks in retainers, plus a damn good chance of ending up in the coop for obstructing justice. As I put Fred's check on my desk the phone rang. It was Mrs. Yeager. She wanted to know when I was going to take her to see the room on 82nd Street. She also wanted to tell me that the daughter of the superintendent of that house had been murdered, and she thought Wolfe and I should look into it. I could do that when I took her to see the room, saving a trip. If you think I should have stopped her because phones have extensions and someone might have been on one, you are correct. I tried to. I finally managed without hanging up on her.

By then Fred was there, having been admitted by Fritz. I gave him his check, and Wolfe gave him his instructions, which he took without a blink. The difference in the way he takes Wolfe and the way he takes me is not based on experience. Up in the bower, getting it only from me, he had suspected that I was perching him far out on a limb and he didn't like it. Now, with Wolfe, there was no question of suspecting or not liking. He had got the idea somehow, long ago, that there was absolutely no limit to what Wolfe could do if he wanted to, so of course there was no risk involved. I would like to be present to see his face if and when Wolfe tells him to go to Moscow and tail Khrushchev. When the doorbell rang he got up and moved to a chair over by the bookshelves as I crossed to the hall.

And got a surprise. It was Julia McGee on the stoop, but she wasn't alone. I stepped back in the office and told Wolfe Aiken was with her. He scowled at me, pursed his lips, and nodded, and I went and opened the door and they entered. For a president Aiken was polite. She was only the ex-secretary of his ex–executive vice-president, but he let her precede him in, down the hall, and into the office. Wolfe stood until they were seated, him in the red leather chair and her in the one Fred had vacated.

Aiken spoke. "You sent for Miss McGee. If there

has been a development, you should have notified
me. I have had no word from you. If you have
something to say to Miss McGee, I want to hear it."

Wolfe was regarding him. "I told you Tuesday
night, Mr. Aiken, that it may be that the less you
know of the particulars of my performance the
better. But it can't hurt for you to know about this;
I would almost certainly have informed you of it
before the day was out. Indeed, it is just as well to
have you present." His head turned. "Fred?"

Fred got up and came to the corner of Wolfe's
desk. "Look at Miss McGee," Wolfe told him. Fred
turned for a glance at her and turned back.

"I don't need to," he said.

"You recognize her?"

"Sure. I ought to; she gave me this." He pointed
to his cheek.

"That was Tuesday evening. Had you seen her
before that?"

"Yes, sir. I saw her Sunday evening when I was
covering that house on Eighty-second Street. I saw
her enter the house. At the basement door."

"Did you see her leave?"

"No, sir. She could have left while I was at the
corner, phoning in. I phoned in every hour, as
instructed. Or after I left for the night."

"Did you tell Archie, Tuesday evening, that you
had seen her before?"

"No, sir. She came at me the second she saw me
Tuesday evening, and it was a tangle. After Archie
took her away I got to thinking. It was her I saw
Sunday. I should have told you, but I knew what it
would mean. It would make me a witness in a
murder case, and you know how that is. But this
morning I decided I'd have to. You were paying me

and you were counting on me. So I came and told you."

"How sure are you that you saw Miss McGee, the woman sitting there, enter that house Sunday evening?"

"I'm dead sure. I wouldn't have come and told you if I wasn't. I know what I'm in for now."

"You deserve it. You had vital information, obtained while you were on an assignment from me, and you withheld it for thirty-six hours. I'll deal with that later. Go to the front room and stay there."

As Fred crossed to the door to the front room no eyes but Wolfe's followed him. Aiken's and mine were on Julia McGee. Hers were on a spot in the pattern of the rug, in front of her feet.

When the door had closed behind Fred, Wolfe spoke. "Miss McGee. Why did you kill him?"

"Don't answer," Aiken commanded her. He turned to Wolfe. "You're working for me. As you put it yourself, you are to make every effort to protect the reputation and interests of the corporation. What's that man's name?"

"Fred Durkin."

"Why did you have him watching that house Sunday evening?"

"On behalf of a client. In confidence."

"You have too many clients. You didn't mention it Tuesday evening. You said you had no engagement."

"We were discussing the murder of Yeager, and I had no engagement to investigate that. I'm humoring you, Mr. Aiken. My other engagements are no concern of yours if there is no conflict of interest. Why did you kill Yeager, Miss McGee?"

Aiken jerked his head to tell her not to answer, and jerked it back to Wolfe. "That's just a trick. Granting that Durkin saw her enter that house Sunday evening, that doesn't prove she killed Yeager. He may not have been there. Did Durkin see *him* enter?"

"No. But someone else did. Mr. and Mrs. Cesar Perez. The janitor and his wife. I would advise you not to approach them. They are bereaved. Their daughter died last night. Since you don't want Yeager's connection with that house disclosed, you had better leave them to Mr. Goodwin and me."

"What time did Yeager enter? Before Miss McGee or after?"

"Before. He arrived around seven o'clock. I am humoring you, sir."

"I don't appreciate it. Granting that Durkin saw Miss McGee enter, he didn't see her leave. Are you accusing her of killing Yeager there in that house and carrying his body out to the street and dumping it in the hole?"

"No. I'm not accusing her; I am confronting her with a fact." Wolfe cocked his head. "Mr. Aiken. I'm not turning our association into a conflict instead of a concert; you are. I told you Tuesday evening that the only feasible way to try to protect the reputation and interests of your corporation with any hope of success would be to stop the police investigation of the murder by reaching an acceptable solution of it without involving that room. I dare contrive such a solution and offer it only if I know what actually happened. It is established that Yeager entered that room around seven o'clock that evening, and it is a reasonable assumption that he was still there when Miss McGee arrived. You say my asking her why she killed him was a trick; certainly it was, and an ancient one; the Greeks used it two thousand years ago, and others long before. I'll withdraw that question and try another." He turned. "Miss McGee. Was Mr. Yeager in that room when you entered it Sunday evening?"

She had finished studying the pattern of the rug some time back. Now her eyes left Wolfe to go to Aiken, and his met them. She said nothing, but he did. "All right, answer it."

She looked at Wolfe, straight. "Yes, he was there. His body was. He was dead."

"Where was the body?"

"On the floor. On the carpet."

"Did you touch it? Move it?"

"I only touched his hair, where the hole was. He was on his side with his mouth open."

"What did you do?"

"I didn't do anything. I sat on a chair a few minutes and then left."

"Exactly what time did you leave?"

"I don't know exactly. It must have been about half past nine. It was a quarter past when I got there."

"Yeager expected you at a quarter past nine?"

"No, at nine o'clock, but I was fifteen minutes late."

"You went to take dictation?"

"Yes."

"At nine o'clock Sunday evening?"

"Yes."

Wolfe grunted. "I think I'll ignore that, Miss McGee. It's a waste of time to challenge lies that are immaterial. It would be pointless to poke the fact at you that Mr. Yeager had arranged for the delivery

of caviar and pheasant at midnight. Was there any
indication that there had been a struggle?"

"No."

"Did you see a gun?"

"No."

"Did you take anything from the room when you
left?"

"No."

"Have you ever owned a gun?"

"No."

"Or borrowed one?"

"No."

"Have you ever shot one?"

"No."

"Where did you go when you left the house?"

"I went home. My apartment. On Arbor Street."

"Did you tell anyone of your experience?"

"No. Of course not."

"You didn't tell Mr. Aiken?"

"No."

"Then he didn't know until now that you were
there Sunday evening?"

"No. Nobody knew."

"Do you know what a hypothetical question is?"

"Certainly."

"I submit one. You said Tuesday evening that
you decided your loyalty should be to the corporation, not to Mr. Yeager, so you betrayed him. Then
if—"

"I didn't betray him. I only thought Mr. Aiken
should know."

Wolfe swiveled to the Webster's Unabridged on
its stand, opened it, and found the page. "Betray,
verb, Definition Two: 'To prove faithless or treach-
erous to, as to a trust or one who trusts.'" He closed

the dictionary and wheeled back. "Surely Yeager trusted you not to tell about that room, but you did. Then if—this is the hypothesis—if you went there Sunday evening, not to take dictation, but to participate in activities congenial to that décor, what am I to assume regarding your disposition at that time toward Mr. Yeager and Mr. Aiken? Had you reconsidered and decided your loyalty was to Mr. Yeager?"

It didn't faze her. She didn't chew on it. "My disposition had nothing to do with it. Mr. Yeager asked me to go there to take dictation, and I went." She was darned good. If I hadn't seen that bower I might have had a sliver of doubt myself. She went on. "That trick question you asked me, why I killed him, I want to ask you, why *would* I kill him? Would I go there to take dictation and take a gun to shoot him?"

Wolfe's shoulders went up a fraction of an inch, and down. "I said I'd ignore your purpose in going there, and I shouldn't have brought it up again. It's futile. If you had a reason for killing him, I won't learn it from you. I doubt if I'll learn anything from you. You say you went there, found him dead, and left." He leaned back, closed his eyes, and pushed his lips out. In a moment he pulled them in. Out again, in again. Out and in, out and in.

Aiken spoke. "I have things to ask Miss McGee myself, but they can wait. You have only made it worse, bringing it out that he was killed in that room. I don't think she killed him, and I don't think you do. What are you going to do now?"

No reply. Wolfe was still working his lips. "He didn't hear you," I told Aiken. "When he's doing that he doesn't hear anything or anybody. We're not here."

Aiken stared at him. He transferred the stare to Miss McGee. She didn't meet it.

Wolfe opened his eyes and straightened up. "Miss McGee. Give me the keys. To the door of that house and the elevator."

"Did you hear what I said?" Aiken demanded.

"No. The keys, Miss McGee."

"I said you've made it worse!" Aiken hit the chair arm with a fist. "Yeager dead in that room! She didn't kill him, she had no reason to, but what if she did? Do you call this protecting the interests of my corporation?"

Wolfe ignored him. "The keys, Miss McGee. You have no further use for them, and you're hardly in a position to balk. You have them?"

She opened her bag, the one I had opened Tuesday evening while she was on the floor wrapped in the coverlet, and took out the key fold. I went and got it, looked at the two keys, and handed it to Wolfe. He put it in a drawer, turned to Aiken, and inquired, "How the deuce did you get to head a large and successful corporation?"

The president goggled at him, speechless. Wolfe went on. "You spout and sputter. You say *I* have made it worse. In your business, do you blame subordinates when they expose problems not of their making which must be solved if the business is to prosper? If I hadn't resorted to humbug we wouldn't know that Yeager was killed in that room, whether by Miss McGee or another, and I might have blundered fatally. I pried it out of her by a ruse. I had cause to suspect she was there Sunday evening, but nothing that could be used as a lever

on her, so I fabricated one. I had no client Sunday
evening; Mr. Durkin was not posted at that house;
he wasn't there to see her enter. But now that I
know she did enter, and that Yeager was killed
there—"

"You tricky bastard!" Aiken was on his feet.
"Where's that paper I signed? I want it!"

"Nonsense." Wolfe didn't bother to tilt his head
to look up at him. Conservation of energy. "Sit
down. You hired me, but you can't fire me. I was
already on slippery ground, withholding information; now that I know Yeager was killed in that
room and his body was seen there I am not merely
vulnerable, I am gravely compromised. You are in
no personal jeopardy, but I am. If I had my share of
prudence I would be at my telephone now, speaking
to Mr. Cramer of the police. What are *you* risking?
The repute of your confounded corporation. Pfui.
Sit down and tell me where you were last evening
from nine o'clock to midnight."

Aiken stood, glaring. His jaw was working, and
a cord at the side of his neck was twitching. "It's
none of your damned business where I was last
evening," he said through his teeth. "I warn you,
Wolfe, you're playing a dangerous game. You lie
when you say Durkin wasn't at that house Sunday.
How else did you know Miss McGee was there? You
never have told me how you found out about that
room. And you had keys. Did Durkin go up after
Miss McGee left and find Yeager's body and take it
out and dump it in that hole? I think he did. And
now you're blackmailing me and my corporation,
that's what it amounts to. All right, you had the
handle Tuesday evening and you still have it, but I
warn you."

"Thank you," Wolfe said politely. His head turned. "Miss McGee, where were you last evening from nine o'clock to midnight?"

"Don't answer him," Aiken commanded her. "Don't answer anything. We're going. You can answer me, but not here. Come on."

She looked at him, at Wolfe, and back at him. "But Mr. Aiken, I have to! I have to answer *that*. I told you, I thought that was what he wanted to see me about—that girl, Maria Perez." She didn't pronounce either "Maria" or "Perez" the way they did. "That's why he wants to know where I was last evening." She turned to Wolfe. "I never saw that girl. I never heard of her until I read the paper today. I didn't kill Mr. Yeager and I didn't kill her. I don't know anything about her. Last evening I had dinner with friends and I was there all evening, with them and other people, until after midnight. Their name is Quinn and they live at Ninety-eight West Eleventh Street. I had to tell him that, Mr. Aiken. It's bad enough for me without—I *had* to."

He was focused on Wolfe. "What about the girl?" he demanded.

Wolfe shook his head. "Since I lie, why bother to ask?"

That was the note it ended on. Plenty of times clients have left that office boiling or sore or sulky, but I have never seen one quite as peevish as Aiken. Not, I must admit, without reason. As he said, Wolfe had the handle, and a president is used to having the handle himself. Leaving with Julia McGee, he forgot his manners, leading the way out of the office and down the hall to the door, and when I reached to get his homburg from the rack he snatched it from my hand. Miss McGee was in for a

bad half-hour. I returned to the office and told
Wolfe, "It's a good thing presidents don't sign
corporation checks. He'd get palsy signing one
made out to you. *If.*"

He grunted. "If indeed. You realize that we have
never been so close to catastrophe. And ignominy."

"Yes, sir."

"It is imperative that we find the murderer
before Mr. Cramer finds that room."

"Yes, sir."

"Will Mr. and Mrs. Perez hold out?"

"Yes, sir."

"Tell Fritz to set a place at lunch for Fred. Then
get Saul and Orrie. Here at two-thirty. If they have
other commitments I'll speak to them. I must have
them this afternoon."

"Yes, sir." I moved.

"Wait. That woman, Meg Duncan—presumably
she was at the theater last evening?"

"Presumably. I can find out."

"Until when?"

"The play ends about ten to eleven; then she had
to change. If she made a date with Maria Perez for
eleven-thirty she could have kept it without rush-
ing. Have I missed something?"

"No. We must cover contingencies. Instructions
after you get Saul and Orrie."

I went to the kitchen to tell Fritz.

Chapter 13

May I introduce Mr. Saul Panzer and Mr. Orrie Cather? Mr. Panzer is the one in the red leather chair. Looking at him—his big nose, his little deepset eyes, his hair that won't stay in place—you will suppose that he isn't much. Hundreds of people who had supposed that have regretted it. A good operative has to be good in a dozen different ways, and in all of them Saul is the best. Mr. Cather, in the yellow chair to Saul's left, might fool you too. He is fully as handsome as he looks, but not quite as smart as he looks, though he might be if his ego didn't get in the way. If a man is to be judged by a single act and you have a choice, the one to pick is how he looks at himself in a mirror, and I have seen Orrie do that. You have met Mr. Fred Durkin, in the chair next to Orrie's.

Wolfe and Fred and I had just come from the dining room to join Saul and Orrie in the office. During lunch I had been wondering what Wolfe had on the program for them, considering the instructions he had given me. With me it had got to the point where earning a fee was only secondary; the main question was how we were going to wriggle down off the limb we were out on; and while I fully appreciated the talents and abilities of those three men, I couldn't guess how they were going to be used to find an answer to that. So I wanted to hear that briefing, but as I went to my chair and whirled it around Wolfe spoke.

"We won't need you, Archie. You have your instructions."

I sat. "Maybe I can supply details."

"No. You had better get started."

I got up and went. There were several pointed remarks I could have made, for instance that I had a right to know what the chances were that I would sleep in my bed that night, but it might not fit his script, granting that he had one, for Saul and Fred and Orrie to know how bad it was. So I went, spry and jaunty until I was in the hall out of sight.

I had a date with an actress, made on the phone, but not for a specified minute—any time between three and four. It was five after three when I entered the lobby of the Balfour on Madison Avenue in the Sixties, gave the hallman my name, and said Miss Meg Duncan was expecting me. He gave me a knowing look and inquired, "How's the fat man?" I said, "Turn around. I'm not much good at faces, but I remember backs." He said, "You wouldn't remember mine. I used to hop at the Churchill. Has Miss Duncan lost something?"

"Questions answered while I wait," I told him. "Mr. Wolfe is just fine, thanks. Miss Duncan can't find her solid gold knuckle-duster and thinks you took it."

He grinned. "It's a treat to meet you. You can pick it up on your way out. Twelfth floor. Twelve D."

I went and entered the elevator and was lifted.

Twelve D was at the end of the hall. I pushed the button, and in half a minute the door opened a crack and a voice asked who it was. I pronounced my name, the door swung wide, and a square-jawed female sergeant gave me an unfriendly look. "Miss Duncan has a bad headache," she said in a voice that went with a jaw and the look. "Can't you tell me what—"

"Mike!" A voice from inside somewhere. "Is that Mr. Goodwin?"

"Yes! He says it is!"

"Then send him in here!"

A man is bound to feel a little uneasy if he has an appointment to call on a young woman in the middle of the afternoon and is ushered into a room dimmed by venetian blinds, and she is in bed and clad accordingly, especially if as soon as the door is closed behind you she says, "I haven't got a headache, sit here," and pats the edge of the bed. Even if you are certain that you can keep control of the situation—but that's the trouble; you can't help feeling that keeping control of the situation is not what your fellow men have a right to expect of you, let alone her fellow women.

There was a chair turned to face the bed, and I took it. As I sat she asked if I had brought her cigarette case.

"No," I said, "but it's still there in the safe, and that's something. Mr. Wolfe sent me to ask you a question. Where were you yesterday evening from nine o'clock to midnight?"

If she had been on her feet, or even on a chair, I believe she would have jumped me again, from the way her eyes flashed. It was personal, not professional. "I wish I had clawed your eyes out," she said.

"I know, you said that before. But I didn't come to fire that question at you just to hear you say it again. If you have seen a newspaper you may have noticed that a girl named Maria Perez was murdered last night?"

"Yes."

"And that she lived at One-fifty-six West Eighty-second Street?"

"Yes."

"So where were you?"

"You know where I was. At the theater. Working."

"Until ten minutes to eleven. Then you changed. Then?"

She was smiling. "I don't know why I said that about clawing your eyes out. I mean I do know. Holding me so tight my ribs hurt, and then just a cold fish. Just a—a stone."

"Not a fish *and* a stone. In fact, neither. Just a detective on an errand. I still am. Where did you go when you left the theater?"

"I came down and went to bed. Here." She patted the bed. The way she used her hands had been highly praised by Brooks Atkinson in the *Times*. "I usually go somewhere and eat something, but last night I was too tired."

"Had you ever seen Maria Perez? Ever run into her in that basement hall?"

"No."

"I beg your pardon; I doubled up the questions. Had you ever seen her or spoken with her?"

"No."

I nodded. "You would say that, naturally, if you thought you could make it stick. But you may have to eat it. This is how it stands. The police haven't got onto that room yet. They still haven't connected Yeager with that house. Mr. Wolfe hopes they won't, for reasons that don't matter to you. He believes that whoever killed Yeager killed Maria Perez, and so do I. He wants to find the murderer and clear it up in such a way that that house doesn't come into it. If he can do that you'll never have to go on the witness stand and identify your cigarette case. But he can do that only if he gets the facts, and gets them quick."

I left the chair and went and sat on the bed where she had patted it. "For example, you. I don't mean facts like where were you Sunday night. We haven't the time or the men to start checking alibis. I asked you about last night just to start the conversation. Your alibi for last night is no good, but it wouldn't have been even if you had said you went to Sardi's with friends and ate a steak. Friends can lie, and so can waiters."

"I was at a benefit performance at the Majestic Theater Sunday night."

"It would take a lot of proving to satisfy me that you were there without a break if I had a healthy reason to think you killed Yeager—but I'm not saying you didn't. An alibi, good or bad, isn't the kind of fact I want from you. You say you never saw or spoke with Maria Perez. Last night her mother phoned me to come, and I went, and searched her room, and hidden under a false bottom in a drawer I found a collection of items. Among them were three photographs of you. Also there was some money, five-dollar bills, that she hadn't wanted her parents to know about. I'm being frank with you, Miss Duncan; I've told you that Mr. Wolfe would prefer to close it up without the police ever learning about that room and the people who went there. But if they do learn about it, not from us, then look out. Not only that you walked in on Mr. and Mrs. Perez and me, and your cigarette case, but what if they find your fingerprints on those five-dollar bills?"

That was pure dumb luck. I would like to say that I had had a hunch and was playing it, but if I once started dolling up these reports there's no telling where I'd stop. I was merely letting my tongue go. If there was anything more in Meg Duncan than the fact (according to her) that she had gone straight home from the theater last night, I wanted to talk it out of her if possible. It was just luck that I didn't mention that the photographs were magazine and newspaper reproductions and that I tossed in the question about the bills.

Luck or not, it hit. She gripped my knee with one of the hands she used so well and said, "My God, the bills. Do they show fingerprints?"

"Certainly."

"Where are they?"

"In the safe in Mr. Wolfe's office. Also the photographs."

"I only gave her one. You said three."

"The other two are from magazines. When did you give it to her?"

"I—I don't remember. There are so many . . ."

My left hand moved to rest on the coverlet where her leg was, above her knee, the fingers bending, naturally, to the curve of the surface they were touching. Of course it would have been a mistake if I had given the hand a definite order to do that, but I hadn't. I'm not blaming the hand; it was merely taking advantage of an opportunity that no alert hand could be expected to ignore; but it got a quicker and bigger reaction than it had counted on. When that woman had an impulse she wasted no time. As she came up from the pillow I met her, I guess on the theory that she was going to claw, but her arms clamped around my neck and she took me back with her, and there I was, on top of her from the waist up, my face into the pillow. She was biting the side of my neck, not to hurt, just cordial.

The time, the place, and the girl is a splendid combination, but it takes all three. The place was okay, but the time wasn't, since I had other errands, and I doubted if the girl's motives were pure. She was more interested in a cigarette case, a photograph, and some five-dollar bills than in me. Also I don't like to be bullied. So I brought my hand up, slipped it between her face and my neck, shoved her head into the pillow while raising mine, folded the ends of the pillow over, and had her smothered. She squirmed and kicked for ten seconds and then stopped. I got my feet on the floor and my weight on them, removed my hands from the pillow, and stepped back. I spoke.

"When did you give her the photograph?"

She was panting, gasping, to catch up on oxygen. When she could she said, "Damn you, you put your hand on me."

"Yeah. Do you expect me to apologize? Patting a place on the bed for me to sit and you in that gauzy thing? You know darned well your nipples show through it. That wasn't very smart, trying to take my mind off of my work when you've got as much at stake as I have." I sat on the chair. "Look, Miss Duncan. The only way you can possibly get clear is by helping Nero Wolfe wrap it up, and we haven't got all summer. We may not even have all day. I want to know about the photograph and the five-dollar bills."

She had got her breath back and pulled the coverlet up to her chin. "You did put your hand on me," she said.

"Conditional reflex. The wonder is it wasn't both hands. When did you give her the photograph?"

"A long time ago. Nearly a year ago. She sent a note to my dressing room at a Saturday matinee. The note said she had seen me at her house and she would like to have three tickets for next Saturday so she could bring two friends. At the bottom below her name was her address. That address . . . I had her sent in. She was incredible. I have never seen a girl as beautiful. I thought she was—that she had been . . ."

I nodded. "A guest in that room. I don't think so."

"Neither did I after I talked with her. She said she had seen me in the hall—twice, she said—and she had recognized me from pictures she had seen. She said she had never told anyone, and she wouldn't, and I gave her an autographed picture and the three tickets. That was in June, and in July we closed for a month for summer vacation, and in August she came to see me again. She was even more beautiful, she was incredible. She wanted three more tickets, and I said I'd mail them to her, and then she said she had decided she ought to have hush money. That's what she said, hush money. Five dollars a month. I was to mail it to her the first of each month, to a branch post office on Eighty-third Street, the Planetarium Station. Have you ever seen her?"

"Yes."

"Then aren't you surprised?"

"No. I quit being surprised after two years of detective work, long ago."

"I was. A girl as beautiful and proud as she was—my God, she was proud. And of course I—well, I supposed that would be only a start. Ever since then I have been expecting her to come again, to tell me she had decided five dollars a month wasn't enough, but she never did."

"You never saw her again?"

"No, but she saw me. She had told me what she did; when she heard the street door open she put out the light in her room and opened the door a crack, and after that when I went there I saw it when I went down the hall, her door open a little. It gave me a feeling—I don't know why—it made it more *exciting* that she was there looking at me." She patted the bed. "Sit here."

I stood up. "No, ma'am. It's even more of a strain when you have the cover up like that, because I know what's under it. I have chores to do. How many five-dollar bills did you send her?"

"I didn't count. It was in August, so the first one was September first, and then every month." The coverlet slipped down.

"Including May? Twelve days ago?"

"Yes."

"That makes nine. They're in Mr. Wolfe's safe. I told Mrs. Perez she'd get them back some day, but since they were hush money you have a valid claim." I took a step, stretched an arm, curved my fingers around her leg, and gave it a gentle squeeze. "See? Conditioned reflex. I'd better go." I turned and walked out. Mike, the female sergeant, appeared from somewhere as I reached the foyer, but let me open the door myself. Down in the lobby I took a moment to tell the hallman, "You can relax. We found them in her jewel box. The maid thought they were earrings." It pays to be on sociable terms with lobby sentries. As I emerged to the sidewalk my watch said 3:40, so Wolfe would be in the office, and I found a phone booth down the block and dialed.

His voice came. "Yes?" He will not answer the phone properly.

"Me. In a booth on Madison Avenue. Money paid to a blackmailer is recoverable, so those bills belong to Meg Duncan. Maria Perez spotted her in the hall a year ago and went to see her and bled her for nine months, five bucks per month. One of the biggest operations in the history of crime. Meg Duncan worked last night and went straight home from the theater and went to bed. I saw the bed and sat on it. Probably true, say twenty to one. From here it's only about eight minutes to the Yeager house. Shall I go there first?"

"No. Mrs. Yeager phoned, and I told her you would be there between five and six. She expects you to take her to see that room. Your problem."

"Don't I know it. You said when I called in you might want to send me to Saul or Fred or Orrie."

"I thought it possible, but no. Proceed."

As I went out to the curb to flag a taxi I was reflecting on Maria's practical horse sense and fine feeling. If you happen to have an autographed photograph of a person whom you are screwing for hush money, you don't keep it. The autographer had of course written something like "Best regards" or "All good wishes," and now that she was your victim it wouldn't be right to hang on to it.

Chapter 14

I had no appointment with Mr. or Mrs. Austin Hough, because, first, I hadn't known when I would finish with Meg Duncan, and second, I preferred to have one of them alone, it didn't matter which. So when I pushed the button in the vestibule at 64 Eden Street I didn't know if there would be anyone at home. There was. The click came; I opened the door and entered, and mounted the stairs. I wasn't awaited at the door of the apartment as before; he was standing at the top of the second flight. As I reached the landing he backed up a step. He wasn't glad to see me.

"Back again," I said politely. "Did you find your wife yesterday?"

"What do you want?" he demanded.

"Nothing startling. A couple of questions. There has been a development that complicates it a little. You probably know about it, the murder of a girl named Maria Perez."

"No. I haven't been out today. I haven't seen a paper. Who is Maria Perez?"

"Not is, was. Then the radio?"

"I haven't turned it on. Who was she?"

"The daughter of the man you saw when you went to that house on Eighty-second Street. Her body was found last night on a North River pier. She was killed, shot, between nine o'clock and midnight. Mr. Wolfe is wondering how you spent the evening. And your wife."

"Balls," he said.

My brows went up in astonishment. He certainly hadn't got that from Robert Browning, though an Elizabethan dramatist might have used it that way. I wasn't up on Elizabethan dramatists. Wherever he had got it, this was a different Austin Hough from the one I had felt sorry for yesterday afternoon—not only that word so used, but his face and bearing. This Hough wasn't asking any favors.

"So," he said, "you want to know how my wife spent last evening? You'd better ask her. Come on." He turned and headed down the hall, and I followed. The door was open. There was no foyer inside. The room, not large, had the furniture of a living room, but the walls were all books. He crossed to a door at the far end, opened it, and motioned me in. Two steps from the sill I stopped dead.

He had killed her. Granting that you shouldn't jump to conclusions, you often do, and for the second time that afternoon I saw a young woman in bed, only this one was completely covered, including her head. Not by a coverlet; a plain white sheet followed her contours, and as we entered there was no sign of movement. A corpse. I stood and stared, but Hough, passing me, spoke.

"It's Archie Goodwin, Dinah. A girl was murdered last night." He turned to me. "What was her name?"

"Maria Perez."

He turned back. "Maria Perez. She lived in that house. Goodwin wants to know what you were doing last evening between nine o'clock and midnight, and I thought you had better tell him. He saw you there in that house yesterday, so I thought he might as well see you now."

Her voice came from beneath the sheet, a mumble that I wouldn't have recognized. "No, Austin, I won't."

"But you will. Don't start it again." He was only a step from the bed. He took it, reached for the top of the sheet, and pulled it back.

I have seen better-looking corpses. The right side of her face was far from normal, but it was nothing compared to the left side. The eye was swollen shut, and the swollen cheek and jaw were the color of freshly sliced calves' liver. Her best curves, of her wide, full mouth, were puffy folds of purple. She was on her back. Her garment had just straps, no sleeves, and from the appearance of her shoulders and upper arms she couldn't have been on her side. I couldn't tell where her one eye was aimed.

Hough, one hand holding the sheet, turned to me. "I told you yesterday," he said, "that I wanted her to know I knew, but I couldn't tell her. I was afraid of what would happen if I told her. Now it has happened." He turned to her. "He wants to know where you were between nine o'clock and midnight. Tell him and he'll go."

"I was here." It was a mumble, but I got it. "Where I am now. By nine o'clock I was like this."

"Your husband left you here like this?"

"He didn't leave me. He was here with me."

"Balls," Hough said, to me. "I came here when I left you and Wolfe, and she was here, and I haven't been out of here since. Now you have seen her, and she has told you, and you can go."

"She's your wife, not mine," I said, "but has a doctor seen her?"

"No. I was filling the ice bags when you rang the bell."

I made my eyes go to her. "Shall I send a doctor, Mrs. Hough?"

"No," she said.

"Send her a bottle of champagne," he said.

And I did. That is, I sent champagne, but not to her, on impulse. When I went to Seventh Avenue to get a taxi, after I had phoned Wolfe to report on the Houghs and tell him I was on my way to Mrs. Yeager, I saw a liquor store and went in and asked if he happened to have a bottle of Dom Pérignon, and he did. I told him to send it to Mr. Austin Hough, 64 Eden Street, and enclose a card on which I wrote "With the compliments of Archie Goodwin." Preferring to make it a personal matter, I didn't put it on expense. I have often wondered whether he dumped it in the garbage, or drank it himself, or shared it with her.

When I left the taxi in front of 340 East 68th Street, at two minutes past five, I stood for a glance around before going to the entrance. Here was where it had started three days ago. There was where the NYPD car had been double-parked with Purley Stebbins' driver in it. Around the corner was the lunchroom where I had phoned Lon Cohen. As I entered the vestibule to push the button I asked myself, if I had known what was ahead would I have given Mike Collins the extra forty bucks?

But I didn't answer because I didn't know what was still ahead.

I didn't know how Wolfe felt about it, but I was more interested in where Mrs. Yeager had been last night than in any of the others. Of course inheriting widows of murdered men always deserve attention, and not only that, she had known that Yeager was nor merely two-timing her, he was twenty-timing her. Her shrugging it off was noble if true, and a good line if false. Her wanting to see that room was natural if true, and again a good line if she had seen it before, Sunday night, when she went there to kill him. Her alibi as published, that she had been in the country and hadn't returned to town until Monday morning, might already have been found leaky by the cops. I suspected that it had, since Cramer had had a tail on her yesterday.

One point in her favor, she wasn't in bed. A uniformed maid showed me through an arch into a living room that would have held six of the Houghs', and in a couple of minutes our Client Number Four appeared. I stood. She stopped just inside the arch and said, "So you're on time. Come on." She had a hat on, and a fur stole, not the mink.

"Are we going somewhere?" I asked, approaching.

"Certainly. You're going to show me that room. The car's waiting."

"I'm afraid this isn't a good time, Mrs. Yeager. After what has happened. Sit down and I'll tell you why."

"You can tell me in the car. You said yesterday you'd take me as soon as you got a chance."

"I know. I tried to get you on the phone at ten

o'clock last evening but couldn't. You weren't at home?"

"Certainly I was. My son and daughter were here, and some friends." She moved. "Come on."

"Damn the torpedoes!" I told her back.

She whirled. For a lump she whirled well. "What did you say?"

"I said damn the torpedoes. That may be your attitude, but it's not Mr. Wolfe's or mine. I came to tell you why we can't go there now. Since the janitor of that house had a daughter, and last night—"

"I know about that. I told you on the phone. She was murdered."

"Right. And it seems likely that she was murdered by the person who murdered your husband. Incidentally, you may remember that Mr. Wolfe suggested the possibility that you killed your husband, so he thinks it's also possible that you killed Maria Perez. That's why I asked if you were at home last evening. Were you here with your son and daughter and friends all evening? Up to midnight?"

"Yes. I said yesterday, it was years ago that I felt like killing him. You're not complete fools, are you?"

"Not complete, no. All right, you didn't kill him. Or her. Some day I'll be glad to take you to see that room, but not now. It's too risky. A girl who lived there has been murdered, and at any time, day or night, a policeman or assistant district attorney may be there to ask questions of her parents or some of the tenants. There may be a man on the outside to keep an eye on the house. If either you or I was seen entering or inside that house, let alone both of us, good-by. Good-by not only to the job Aiken hired Wolfe for, but also to the one you hired him for. Another thing, you are probably still being followed around."

"They wouldn't dare."

"Wouldn't they, though. They did, didn't they? We'll have to postpone it. The room will keep."

"Are you going to take me there or not?"

"Not now. Not today."

"I thought so. There is no such room."

"Oh yes there is. I've seen it. Several times."

"I don't believe it." Her sharp little eyes were slanted up to mine. "Benedict Aiken invented it, or Nero Wolfe did, or you did. You've been making a fool of me. I suspected it yesterday, and now I know it. Get out of my house. I'm going to call the District Attorney."

I was observing an interesting fact, that two chins can look fully as determined as one. I couldn't possibly talk her out of it, and there was no use trying. I made one stab at it.

"You're looking at me, Mrs. Yeager. Our eyes are meeting. Do I look like a liar?"

"Yes."

"Okay, then you'll have to be shown. You say your car's waiting. With a chauffeur?"

"Certainly."

"Nothing doing. If this house is covered he wouldn't even have to follow to find out where we went unless the chauffeur is a hero. We'll leave together, that doesn't matter, and walk to Second Avenue. You'll wait at the corner, and when I come in a taxi you'll get in. I'll show you whether there's such a room or not."

The sharp little eyes were suspicious. "Is this another trick?"

"Why ask me, since I'm a liar? Sure, I'm kidnaping you. In my circle we call it a snatch."

It took her four seconds to decide. "All right, come on," she said, and moved.

Out on the sidewalk she stopped to speak to the chauffeur standing beside a black Lincoln, and then went with me to the corner. From there on I took the standard routine precautions, going uptown a block to get a taxi, and picking her up at the corner. I had the hackie do turns until I was sure we were unaccompanied and then drop us on Madison Avenue in the Seventies. When he was out of sight I flagged another taxi, told the driver 82nd and Amsterdam, and when we got there told him to crawl the block to Columbus. At Columbus, having seen no sign of a city employee, I told him to take 81st Street back to Amsterdam and stop at the corner. There I paid him off and took Mrs. Yeager into a drugstore and, since she suspected tricks, I had her come along to the phone booth and stand at my elbow while I dialed a number and talked. What she heard:

"Mrs. Perez? This is Archie Goodwin. I'm in a drugstore around the corner. I hope we're still friends? . . . Good. Has a policeman been there? . . . You didn't? Good. . . . No, that's all right, taking you downtown and having you sign a statement was normal, they always do. Is anyone there now? . . . Okay. I'm coming there with a woman, we'll be there in two minutes, and I'm taking her up in the elevator. We won't be there long. I may phone you this evening, or I may drop in. . . . No, but I hope there soon will be. . . . Absolutely. I'm your detective."

As I hung up Mrs. Yeager demanded, "Who was that?"

"The mother of the girl who was murdered last night. Since you didn't kill her there's no conflict of interest. Let's go."

We walked the block to 82nd, around the corner, on to Number 156, and in at the basement door. There was no one in the hall, and the door of Maria's room was shut. At the elevator I used the second key and we entered.

Not being a psychologist or a sociologist, I wouldn't know how a middle-aged widow with a double chin is supposed to react on entering a bower that her husband had used for extramarital activities, but whatever the pattern is I'll give any odds you name that Mrs. Thomas G. Yeager didn't follow it. When I switched on the lights she took a couple of steps, stopped, moved her head slowly around to the right, moved it back more slowly and to the left, and turned to face me.

"I apologize," she said.

"Accepted," I said. "Forget it."

She took a few more steps, stopped for another look around, and turned again. "No bathroom?"

I believe it only because I heard it. You haven't that privilege. "Sure," I said, "at the far end. The kitchen's at this end." I pointed. "That gold push plate is on the door." I swung my arm around. "There where the silk is tucked; it's a curtain. Drawers behind it."

That ended the conversation, though her inspection took more than half an hour. First she took in the pictures, not collectively, one by one, moving along, tilting her head back for the high ones. No comment. When she slid the curtain aside and began opening drawers I went to a chair and sat. She took nothing out of the drawers and didn't poke in them. She stooped over for a close look at the carpet. She examined the upholstery on the chairs and couches. She twisted her neck up and around to survey the indirect-lighting installation. She pulled the top of the bed coverlet down to see the linen and put it neatly back again. She was in the kitchen a good five minutes, and in the bathroom longer. She did the bathroom last, and when she came out she got her stole from the couch where she had put it, and spoke.

"Do you believe that Julia McGee came here to take dictation?"

"No." I rose. "Do you?"

"Certainly not. Why do you think the person who killed my husband killed that girl?"

"It's complicated. But it's not just a guess."

"Where's her mother? I want to speak to her."

"Better not, right now." I was moving toward the elevator, and she was coming. "It hit her pretty hard. Some other day." I pushed the button, the elevator door opened, and we entered

Just to get it straight for my own satisfaction, I have tried to figure exactly where we were when the doorbell rang in the basement. We must have been either entering the elevator or on our way down. Anyhow, I didn't hear it, so we emerged below and started up the hall. When we were about halfway to the front Mrs. Perez came out of a door ahead on the right, the one she and Maria had come out of when her husband called her my first time there, went to the street door, and opened it. As I say, I hadn't heard the doorbell, so I supposed she was going out. But she wasn't. Mrs. Yeager and I

were right there when Sergeant Purley Stebbins
said, "Sorry to bother you again, Mrs. Perez,
but—" saw us, and stopped.

A mind can do crazy things. Mine, instead of
instantly tackling the situation, took a tenth of a
second to tell me how lucky I was that Stebbins
hadn't been already inside and with Mrs. Perez in
the hall when we stepped out of the elevator. That
helped a lot, to know I was lucky.

"You?" Stebbins said. He crossed the sill. "And
you, Mrs. Yeager?"

"We were just leaving," I said. "Having had a
talk with Mrs. Perez."

"What about?"

"About her daughter. I suppose you know that
Mrs. Yeager has hired Mr. Wolfe to find out who
killed her husband. She told Cramer yesterday. She
has some detective instincts herself. When she read
in the paper today that a girl named Maria Perez
had been murdered, shot in the head, and she had
lived in this street, in the block where Yeager's
body had been found, and her body had been taken
somewhere and dumped just as Yeager's had been,
she got the idea that there was some connection
between the two murders. Mr. Wolfe thought it was
possible, and so did I. Mrs. Yeager's idea was that
Maria Perez might have seen the murderer dumping Yeager's body in the hole, maybe from the
sidewalk as she was coming home, or maybe even
from inside, from a window. Of course there were
difficulties, but Mr. Wolfe thought it wouldn't hurt
for me to have a talk with Maria's mother or father,
and Mrs. Yeager wanted to come along. It would be
a coincidence if you came with the same idea just as
we were leaving. Wouldn't it?"

As I was reeling it off I knew how bad it was. First, because it was full of holes, and second, because it wasn't me. When Stebbins barked at me a question like "What about?" my natural answer would be "The weather" or something similar, and he knew it. It was against all precedent for me to oblige with a long, detailed explanation, but I had to, for Mrs. Yeager and Mrs. Perez. It was probably up the flue anyway, but there was a chance that they would catch on and help me save the pieces.

Actually it wasn't as bad as I thought. I knew so much about that house and that room that I didn't sufficiently consider that Stebbins knew nothing whatever about it, that Homicide and the DA had been assuming for three days that Yeager had been killed elsewhere and brought and dumped in that hole because it was convenient, and they had absolutely no reason to connect him with that house. And Mrs. Yeager came through like an angel. She couldn't have done better if I had spent an hour priming her. She offered a hand to Mrs. Perez and said in exactly the right tone, "Thank you, Mrs. Perez. We have both lost someone dear to us. I have to go, I'm late now. We didn't intend to keep you so long and it was very kind of you. I'll phone you later, Mr. Goodwin, or you call me." The door was standing open, and out she went. I could have kissed her on both chins.

Stebbins was eying me as if he would like to kick me on both butts, but that was only normal. "What did you ask Mrs. Perez and what did she tell you?" he demanded. He was hoarse, but that was normal too. Wolfe and I both have that effect on him, Wolfe more than me.

It was a good question. The way I had sketched it, we had come to ask Mrs. Perez about her daughter's whereabouts and movements Sunday night, and presumably she had told us; and I had no idea where Maria had been Sunday night. An excellent question. So I reverted to type. "What do you suppose I asked her? I wanted to know if it was possible that her daughter had seen someone dumping Yeager's body in that hole and climbing in to put the tarp over him. As for what she said, get the *best* evidence. She's here. Ask her."

"I'm asking you." Stebbins is not a fool.

"And I'm reserving my answer. I don't owe Mrs. Perez anything, but she has a right to decide for herself what she wants to say for the official record. Mrs. Yeager and I were merely people. You're a cop."

And by gum Mrs. Perez came through too. Not as grand a performance as Mrs. Yeager's, but plenty good enough. "What I told him was just the truth," she told Stebbins. "If my daughter saw anything like that Sunday she would tell me, so she didn't."

"Was she home all evening?"

"Yes. Two of her friends came and they watched television."

"What time did the friends come?"

"It was about eight o'clock."

"What time did they leave?"

"Right after eleven o'clock. Right after a program they like every Sunday night."

"Did your daughter go out with them?"

"No."

"Did she leave the house at all that evening?"

"No."

"Are you sure?"

She nodded. "I'm sure. We always knew where she was."

"You didn't know last night. And any time during the night, Sunday night, she could have gone to the front room and looked out through the window. Couldn't she?"

"Why would she? Why would she do that?"

"I don't know, but she could." Stebbins turned. "All right, Goodwin, I'll ride you downtown. You can tell the inspector about it."

"About what? What is there to tell?"

He stuck his chin out. "Look, you. Monday afternoon you began checking on a man that was already dead, two hours before the body was found. When the inspector goes to see Wolfe he finds the widow there, and he gets the usual crap. The widow has hired Wolfe to find out who killed her husband, which may not be against the law but it's against the policy of the New York Police Department. And I come here investigating not that murder but another one, and by God here you are, you *and* the widow, here in the house where that girl lived, talking with her mother. So you're coming downtown or you're under arrest as a material witness."

"Am I under arrest?"

"No. I said *or*."

"It's nice to have a choice." I got a quarter from my pocket, flipped it in the air, caught it, and looked at it. "I win. Let's go."

It suited me fine to get him away from Mrs. Perez and out of that house. As I mounted the three steps to the sidewalk I was thinking how different

it would be if he had come thirty seconds sooner or
we had left the bower thirty seconds later. As I
climbed in the PD car I yawned, thoroughly. Having
had less than three hours' sleep, I had been needing
a good healthy yawn all day but had been too busy.

Chapter 15

Six hours later, at one-thirty in the morning, I was sitting in the kitchen, putting away black bread (made by Fritz), smoked sturgeon, Brie cheese, and milk, and reading the early edition of Friday's *Times*, which I had picked up on my way home from the District Attorney's office.

I was about pooped. The day had been fairly active, and the evening, an hour with Cramer and four hours with a couple of assistant DAs, had been really tough. It's a strain to answer a thousand questions put by experts when you know that: a) you have to keep a wall between two sets of facts, the ones they already know and the ones you hope to God they never will know; b) you're making a record that may hook you on a charge you can't possibly dodge; and c) one little slip could spill the soup. Of all the sessions I have had at Homicide West and the DA's office, that was the worst. There had been only two letups, when they called time out for ten minutes for me to eat an inedible ham sandwich and a pint of Grade F milk, and when I announced, around ten o'clock, that they could either let me make a phone call or lock me up for the night.

Anyone who thinks the phone booths in that building are not tapped has a right to his opinion, but so have I. Therefore when I got Wolfe and told him where I was we kept it on a high plane. I reported the encounter with Stebbins and said that as usual Cramer and the DA thought I was withholding information they had a right to, which, as he knew, was absurd. He said that he already knew of the encounter with Stebbins, that Mrs. Yeager had phoned and he had requested her to come to the office, and they had discussed the matter. He asked if it would be advisable for Fritz to keep the casseroled kidneys warm, and I said no, I was on a diet. They finally turned me loose at a quarter to one, and when I got home the house was dark and there was no note on my desk.

When I had taken on a satisfactory amount of the bread and sturgeon and cheese, and learned from the *Times* that the District Attorney hoped he would soon be able to report progress in the Yeager murder investigation, I dragged myself up the two flights to my room. I had promised my dentist years ago that I would brush my teeth every night, but that night I skipped it.

Since I had done all my errands and there had been no note on my desk, and I was behind on sleep, I didn't turn the radio alarm on, and when I pried my eyes open enough to see the clock it said 9:38. Wolfe would have finished breakfast and gone up to the orchids. I thought another ten minutes wouldn't hurt, but I hate to dash around in the morning fog, so I turned on my will power and rolled out. At 10:17 I entered the kitchen, told Fritz good morning, and got my orange juice. At 10:56 I finished my second cup of coffee, thanked Fritz for the bacon and apricot omelet, went to the office, and started opening the mail. The sound came of the elevator and Wolfe entered, said good morning, went to his desk, and asked if there was any word from Hewitt about the Lycaste delicatissima. True to form. Granting that he knew they hadn't tossed me in the can as a material witness, since I was there, and that I had nothing urgent to report, since I wouldn't have waited until eleven o'clock, he might at least have asked how long they had kept me. Slitting envelopes, I said there was nothing from Hewitt.

"How long did they keep you?" he asked.

"Only three hours more after I phoned. I got home a little after one."

"It must have been rather difficult."

"There were spots. I refused to sign a statement."

"That was wise. Satisfactory. Mrs. Yeager told me of your impromptu explanation to Mr. Stebbins. She was impressed. Satisfactory."

Two satisfactories in one speech was a record. "Oh," I said, "just my usual discretion and sagacity. It was either that or shoot him." I took the mail to him. "Anything on the program?"

"No. We are suspended." He pushed the buzzer button, one long and one short, for beer, and got at the mail. In a moment Fritz came with a bottle and a glass. I sat and yawned, and got my notebook out. There would be letters. The phone rang. It was Lon Cohen, wanting to know if I had spent a pleasant evening at the DA's office and how had I got bail in the middle of the night. I told him bail wasn't permitted on a murder one charge; I had jumped out a window and was now a fugitive. When I hung up Wolfe was ready to dictate, but as I picked up my notebook and swiveled, the phone rang again. It was Saul Panzer. He wanted Wolfe. Wolfe didn't give me the off signal, so I stayed on.

"Good morning, Saul."

"Good morning, sir. I've got it. Tight."

"Indeed?"

"Yes, sir. A little place on Seventy-seventh Street near First Avenue. Three-sixty-two East Seventy-seventh Street. His name is Arthur Wenger." Saul spelled it. "He picked him from the photograph and he's positive. He's not sure of the day, but it was last week, either Tuesday or Wednesday, in the morning. I'm in a booth around the corner."

"Satisfactory. I want him here as soon as possible."

"He won't want to come. He's alone in the place. Ten dollars would probably do it, but you know how that is. He'll be asked if he was paid."

"He won't be asked—or if he is, I'll be foundered anyway. Ten dollars, twenty, fifty, no matter. When will you have him here?"

"Half an hour."

"Satisfactory. I'll expect you."

We hung up. Wolfe glanced up at the clock and said, "Get Mr. Aiken."

I dialed Continental Plastic Products. Mr. Aiken was in conference and couldn't be disturbed. I got that not only from a female who was polite, but also from a male who thought *he* shouldn't have been disturbed. The best I could get was that a message would be conveyed to Mr. Aiken within fifteen minutes, and I made the message brief: "Call Nero

Wolfe, urgent." In nine minutes the phone rang and the polite female asked me to put Mr. Wolfe on. I don't like that, even with a president, so I told her to put Mr. Aiken on, and she didn't make an issue of it. In a minute I had him and signed to Wolfe.

"Mr. Aiken? Nero Wolfe. I have a report to make and it's exigent. Not on the telephone. Can you be here with Miss McGee by a quarter past twelve?"

"Not conveniently, no. Can't it wait until after lunch?"

"It shouldn't. Sometimes convenience must bow to necessity. Delay would be hazardous."

"Damn it, I . . ." Pause. "You say with Miss McGee?"

"Yes. Her presence is required."

"I don't know." Pause. "All right. We'll be there."

Wolfe hung up. He cleared his throat. "Your notebook, Archie. Not a letter, a draft of a document. Not for mailing."

Chapter 16

On the wall of the office, at the right as you enter, is a picture of a waterfall, not large, 14 by 17. Its center is one inch below my eye level, but I'm just under six feet tall. The picture was made to order. On the wall of the alcove at the end of the hall is a hinged wood panel. Swing it open, and there's the back of the picture, but your eyes go on through and you are looking into the office. At twenty minutes past twelve the eyes that were doing that belonged to Mr. Arthur Wenger of 362 East 77th Street, a skinny guy past fifty with big ears and not much hair, who had been delivered by Saul Panzer in a little less than the specified half hour. The object in the office nearest him was the red leather chair, and its occupant, Mr. Benedict Aiken.

I wasn't in the alcove with Wenger; Saul was. Wolfe and I were at our desks in the office. Julia McGee was on a yellow chair facing Wolfe's desk. Wolfe was speaking. ". . . but before I submit my conclusion I must tell you how I came by it. When you asked me Tuesday evening who would decide if I have faithfully observed the provision of my employment, I said reason and good faith, applied jointly. You can judge fairly only if you know how I proceeded. Frankly, I am myself not entirely certain. I only know that in the circumstances— Yes, Saul?"

Saul was in the doorway. "It's a perfect fit, Mr. Wolfe."

"Very well. I'll look at it later." Wolfe went back to Aiken. "In the circumstances there was no other course open to me. As I told you, the only way to stop the police investigation of the murder was to reach an acceptable solution of it without involving that room. I have never tackled a task that looked so unpromising. Indeed, knowing as I did that Yeager had been killed in that room, it seemed all but hopeless."

"You didn't know that until you set that trap for Miss McGee yesterday." Aiken was curt.

"No. I knew it much earlier, Tuesday noon, when Mr. Goodwin reported his conversation with Mr. and Mrs. Perez, the janitor of that house and his wife. When Mr. Perez had gone up with refreshments at midnight Sunday he had found the body there, and they had taken it out and put it in that hole."

"They admitted it?"

"They had to. The alternative Mr. Goodwin offered them was worse."

"They killed him. That's obvious. They killed him."

Wolfe shook his head. "That was an acceptable conjecture until yesterday morning, but they didn't kill their daughter—and that's where my report to you begins. That conjecture was then discarded in favor of another, that that girl had been killed by the person who killed Yeager—discarded by me, not by Mr. Goodwin, who had not accepted it. Summoned to that house Wednesday night by Mrs. Perez, he searched the girl's room and found evidence that supported the second conjecture. Archie?"

I went and got Maria's collection from the safe and took it to him.

He tapped it with a fingertip. "This," he said, "is that girl's carefully hidden record of a secret venture that in the end cost her her life. It is all concerned with Thomas G. Yeager. No doubt it was initiated, as so many ventures are, but simple curiosity, stirred by the existence of the elevator and the room which she was not allowed to see. She found that by turning out the light in her room and opening her door a crack she could see visitors bound for the elevator as they came down the hall. I don't know when she first did that, but I do know that, having started, she repeated it frequently."

He picked up the tear sheets. "These are from the financial pages of the *Times*, with the entries for Continental Plastic Products marked with a pencil." He put them aside. "These are advertisements of Continental Plastic Products." He put them with the tear sheets. "Labels from champagne bottles. Mr. Goodwin is of the opinion that Miss Perez drank none of the champagne, and I concur. These items are not essentials, they are merely tassels. So are these: newspaper reproductions of photographs, two of Mr. Yeager, one of his son, and one of his wife. I mention them only to show you how diligent Miss Perez was."

He put them with the other tassels and picked up the pictures of Meg Duncan and the bills. "These two items are of more consequence: nine five-dollar bills, and three pictures of a woman who is a public figure—one from a newspaper and two from magazines. I have spoken with her, and Mr. Goodwin talked with her at length yesterday afternoon. The money was extorted from her by Miss Perez, who had seen her in that house and demanded what she called hush money. The woman sent her five dollars a month for nine months, by mail. There is no need to name her."

He opened a drawer, put the pictures and bills in it, and shut it. "But those items raise a question. Call the woman Miss X. Mr. Yeager arrived at the house Sunday evening around seven o'clock. Miss McGee arrived at a quarter past nine and found him dead. The conjecture was that Miss Perez had seen someone arrive between those hours, had recognized him or her, had concluded that he or she had killed Yeager, had undertaken a more ambitious venture in extortion, and had herself been killed. Then, since she would have recognized Miss X, why not assume that Miss X was the culprit? A reasonable assumption; but it has been established beyond question that Miss X was at a public gathering Wednesday evening until eleven o'clock, and Miss Perez left the motion-picture theater, to keep her appointment with her intended prey, before nine o'clock."

Aiken flipped an impatient hand. "You said this was urgent. What's urgent about proving that a Miss X is out of it?"

"The urgency will appear. This is a necessary prelude to it. Still another reason for excluding not only Miss X, but others: Whoever went there Sunday evening between seven and nine, with a

gun and intending to use it, must have known that
no other visitor would be there. What is true of
Miss X is also true of every other woman who had
keys to that place: First, she couldn't have gone by
invitation, since Miss McGee had been invited, and
Yeager entertained only one guest at a time; and
second, she couldn't have expected to find him alone
there on a Sunday evening—or rather, she could
have expected to find him alone only if she knew
that Miss McGee would arrive at nine o'clock."
Wolfe's head turned. "Miss McGee. Had you told
anyone that you were going there at nine o'clock?"

"No." It came out a squeak and she tried it
again. "No, I hadn't."

"Then the others are excluded as well as Miss X.
Now for you, madam. And the next item in Miss
Perez' collection. These are pencil sketches she
made of women she saw in that hall." He picked
them up. "She was not without talent. There are
thirty-one of them, and they are dated. Mr. Goodwin and I have studied them with care. There are
four sketches each of three women, three each of
five women, two of one woman, and one each of two
women. The one of whom there are two sketches is
you, and one of them is dated May eighth. It gave
me the surmise, which I tricked you into validating,
that you were there Sunday evening. Would you
care to look at it?"

"No." This time it was too loud.

Wolfe put the sketches in the drawer and returned his eyes to Julia McGee. "It was the fact that
those two sketches were in the collection that made
it extremely doubtful that it was you who had killed
Miss Perez, having been threatened with exposure
by her. For there are no sketches of persons whose

names she knew. There are none of Mr. Yeager or Miss X. The sketches are merely memoranda. It is highly likely that she had made one or more of Miss X, but when she had identified her from published pictures she discarded the sketches. If she had identified you, if she knew your name, she would have preserved, not the sketches, but the ground for the identification, as she did with Miss X. Surely she would not have made a second sketch of you when she saw you in the hall Sunday evening."

Aiken snorted. "You don't have to persuade us that Miss McGee didn't kill the girl. Or Yeager."

Wolfe turned to him. "I am describing my progress to my conclusion. It is apparent that Miss Perez had assembled, and was keeping hidden, a complete record of her discoveries regarding Mr. Yeager and the visitors to that room. It is certain that she knew the name of the person whom she saw in the hall between seven and nine Sunday evening, since she was able to reach him, to confront him with her knowledge and her threat. Therefore it was a sound assumption that this collection contained an item or items on which her identification of that person was based."

He pointed to the tassels. "Two such items are there: the pictures of Mr. Yeager's wife and son, with their names. I rejected them because they did not meet the specifications. The person who went there Sunday evening with a gun and shot Yeager with it must have had keys and known how to use them, and he must have known that Miss McGee intended to arrive at nine o'clock, since otherwise he could not have expected to find Yeager alone. It was conceivable that either the wife or son met those requirements, but it was highly improbable."

He picked up the remaining item. "Adopting that reasoning, at least tentatively, I was left with this. This is a picture, reproduced in a magazine, of a gathering in the ballroom of the Churchill Hotel, a banquet of the National Plastics Association. Mr. Yeager is at the microphone. The caption gives the names of the men on the dais with him, including you. No doubt you are familiar with the picture?"

"Yes. I have it framed on the wall of my office."

"Well." Wolfe dropped it on his desk. "I asked myself, what if it was you whom Miss Perez saw in the hall on your way to the elevator Sunday evening between seven and nine? What if, having this picture in her collection, she recognized you? What if, later, having learned that Yeager had been killed up in that room—for she must have seen her father and mother transporting the body—she guessed that you had killed him, decided to make you pay for her silence, communicated with you, made an appointment to meet you, and kept it? You will concede that those were permissible questions."

"Permissible? Yes." Aiken was disdainful. "You don't need permission to ask preposterous questions."

Wolfe nodded. "Of course that was the point. Were they preposterous? To answer that, further questions had to be asked. One, could you have had keys? Two, could you have known Yeager would be there alone? Three, had you a motive?"

Wolfe stuck a finger up. "One. You could have borrowed Miss McGee's keys, but if so you would have had to return them to her before nine o'clock so she could let herself in. That did seem preposterous, that you would return the borrowed keys so she could enter, find Yeager's body, and inevitably assume that you had killed him. Not tenable."

"Do you expect me to sit here and listen to this nonsense?"

"I do. We have arrived at the urgency and you know it." Another finger up. "Two. Yes. You could have known Yeager would be there alone. Miss McGee says she told no one of her nine o'clock appointment, but that was to be expected if it was you she told." Another finger. "Three. When I first asked that question, had you a motive, I knew nothing about it, but I do now. Yesterday I made some inquiries on the telephone—I assure you they were discreet—and last evening Mrs. Yeager sat for an hour in the chair you now occupy and gave me many details. For five years, since he became executive vice-president, Yeager has been a threat to your leadership of the corporation, and in the last year the threat has become ominous and imminent. The best you could expect was that you would be made chairman of the board, removed from active control, and even that was doubtful. Since you had dominated the corporation's affairs for more than ten years, that prospect was intolerable. You can't very well challenge this, since the situation is known to many people."

Wolfe's fingers came down, and his hand dropped to the desk. "But what chiefly concerned me when you and Miss McGee left this room twenty-four hours ago was not your motive; a motive, however deeply hidden, can be exposed. The problem was the keys, and there was an obvious possibility, that you had borrowed Miss

McGee's keys, not last Sunday, but at some previous date, had had duplicates made, and had returned them to her. Testing that possibility would have been hopeless if they had been ordinary keys, but Rabsons are peculiar and there aren't many of them. I decided to try. I sent for three men who help me on occasion and gave them this picture and the keys I got from Miss McGee yesterday. They had copies made of the picture and duplicates of the keys, and returned these to me. They were to start with the locksmiths nearest your home and office. Only a little more than an hour ago, just before I phoned you, one of them, Mr. Saul Panzer, turned the possibility into a fact. This is of course the crux of my report." He pushed a button on his desk. "This begot the urgency."

His eyes went to the door, and Saul appeared with Arthur Wenger. They came to the front of Wolfe's desk and turned to face Aiken. Wolfe said to Aiken, "This is Mr. Arthur Wenger. Do you recognize him?"

Aiken was staring at Wenger. He moved the stare to Wolfe. "No," he said. "I've never seen him."

"Mr. Wenger, this is Mr. Benedict Aiken. Do you recognize him?"

The locksmith nodded. "I recognized him from the picture. It's him all right."

"Where and when have you seen him before?"

"He came to my shop one day last week with a couple of Rabson keys to get duplicates made. He waited while I made them. I think it was Wednesday, but it could have been Tuesday. He's a liar when he says he's never seen me."

"How sure are you?"

"I couldn't be any surer. People are like keys;

they're a lot alike but they're all different. I don't know faces as well as I know keys, but well enough. I look at keys and I look at faces."

"It's an excellent habit. That's all now, sir, but I'll appreciate it if you can spare another hour."

"I said I could."

"I know. I appreciate it."

Saul touched Wenger's arm, and they went. In the hall they turned left, toward the kitchen. Soon after Saul had phoned, Fritz had got started on a chicken pie with forcemeat and truffles for their lunch, and it would soon be ready.

Wolfe leaned back, cupped his hands over the ends of the chair arms, and spoke. "Miss McGee. Manifestly Mr. Aiken is doomed. You shifted your loyalty from Mr. Yeager to him; now you must shift it from him to yourself. You're in a pickle. If he is put on trial you'll be a witness. If you testify under oath that you did not lend him your keys and that you didn't tell him you would arrive at that house at nine o'clock Sunday evening you will be committing perjury, and it may be provable. More and worse: You may be charged as an accessory to murder. You lent him the keys, he had duplicates made, and he used the duplicates to enter a house to kill a man. You made it possible for him to enter the house without hazard, ensuring that Yeager would be alone, by arranging a nine-o'clock assignation—"

"I didn't arrange it!" Too loud again. "Nine o'clock was the usual time! And I only told Mr. Aiken because—"

"Hold your tongue!" Aiken was on his feet, confronting her. "He tricked you once and he's trying it again. We're going. I'm going, and you're going with me!"

I was up. If she had left her chair I would have
moved between them and the door, but she stayed
put. She tilted her head back to look up at him, and
I have never seen a stonier face. "You're a fool," she
said. I have never heard a harder voice. "A bun-
gling old fool. I suspected you had killed him but I
didn't want to believe it. If you had had any
brains—don't stand there glaring at me!" He was
in front of her, and she moved her chair to send her
eyes to Wolfe. "Yes, he borrowed my keys. He said
he wanted to see the room. He had them two days.
And I told him I was going there Sunday night at
nine o'clock. I had promised to keep him informed.
Informed! I was a fool too." Her voice stayed hard
but it was also bitter. "God, what a fool."

Wolfe shook his head. "'Fool' doesn't do you
justice, Miss McGee. Say rather harpy or lamia. I'm
not judging you, merely classifying you. Pfui." He
turned to Aiken. "So much for what is done; now
what to do."

Aiken had returned to the red leather chair.
With his hands, fists, on his thighs, and his jaw
clamped, he was trying to pretend he wasn't licked,
but he knew he was. Knowing what was ahead after
Wolfe had dictated the draft of a document, I had
got the Marley from the drawer and loaded it and
slipped it in my pocket, but now I knew it wouldn't
be needed. I sat down.

Wolfe addressed him. "I am in a quandary. The
simplest and safest course would be to telephone
Mr. Cramer of the police to come and get you. But
under the terms of your employment of me on
behalf of your corporation I am obliged to make
every effort to protect the reputation and interests
of the corporation, and to disclose no facts or

information that will harm the corporation's repute or prestige unless I am compelled to do so by my legal obligation as a citizen and a licensed private detective. That is verbatim. Of course it isn't possible to suppress the fact that the corporation's president murdered its executive vice-president; that isn't discussible. You are doomed. With the evidence I already possess and the further evidence the police would gather, your position is hopeless."

He opened a drawer and took out a paper. "But it may be feasible to prevent disclosure of the existence of that room and Yeager's connection with it, and that was your expressed primary concern when you came here Tuesday night. I doubt if you care much now, but I do. I want to meet the terms of my engagement as far as possible, and with that in mind I prepared a draft of a document for you to sign. I'll read it to you." He lifted the paper and read:

"I, Benedict Aiken, make and sign this statement because it has been made clear to me by Nero Wolfe that there is no hope of preventing disclosure of my malefaction. But I make it of my own free will and choice, under the coercion not of Nero Wolfe but only of the circumstances. On the night of May 8, 1960, I killed Thomas G. Yeager by shooting him in the head. I transported his body to West 82nd Street, Manhattan, and put it in a hole in the street. There was a tarpaulin in the hole, and to postpone discovery of the body I covered it with the tarpaulin. I killed Thomas G. Yeager because he threatened to supersede me in my office of president of Continental Plastic

*Products and deprive me of effective control of
the affairs of the corporation. Since I was
responsible for the development and progress
of the corporation for the last ten years, that
prospect was intolerable. I feel that Yeager
deserved his fate, and I express no regret or
remorse for my deed."*

Wolfe leaned back. "I included no mention of
Maria Perez because that is not essential and it
would require a lengthy explanation, and there is no
danger of an innocent person being held to account
for her death. The police will in time file it, along
with other unsolved problems. You may of course
suggest changes—for example, if you do feel regret
or remorse and wish to say so, I offer no objection."

He held the paper up. "Of course this, written on
my typewriter, will not do. Anyhow, such a document should be a holograph to make it indubitably
authentic, so I suggest that you write it by hand on
a plain sheet of paper, with the date and your
signature. Here and now. Also address an envelope
by hand to me at this address and put a postage
stamp on it. Mr. Panzer will go to a mailbox near
your home and mail it. When he phones that it has
been mailed you will be free to go your way." His
head turned. "Is there any chance that it will be
delivered here today, Archie?"

"No, sir. Tomorrow morning."

He went back to Aiken. "I shall of course
communicate with the police without undue
delay—say around ten o'clock." He cocked his
head. "The advantage to me of this procedure is
obvious; I shall be able to collect a fee from the
corporation; but the advantage to you is no less

clear. Surely it is to be preferred to the only alternative: immediate arrest and constraint, indictment on a murder charge, indeed two murders, disclosure of the existence of that room and of the efforts of yourself and your associates to prevent the disclosure, the ordeal of the trial, the probable conviction. Even if you are not convicted, the years ahead, at your age, are not attractive. I am merely—"

"Shut up!" Aiken barked.

Wolfe shut up. I raised my brows at Aiken. Had he actually, there under the screw, the nerve to think he might tear loose? His face answered me. The bark had come not from nerve, but from nerves, nerves that had had all they could take. I must hand it to him that he didn't wriggle or try to crawl. He didn't even stall, try to get another day or even an hour. He didn't speak; he just put out a hand, palm up. I went and got the document and gave it to him, then got a sheet of typewriter paper and a blank envelope and took them to him. He had a pen; he had taken it from his pocket. His hand was steady as he put the paper on the stand at his elbow, but it shook a little as he put pen to paper. He sat stiff and still for ten seconds, then tried again, and the hand obeyed orders.

Wolfe looked at Julia McGee and said in a voice as hard as hers had been, "You're no longer needed. Go." She started to speak, and he snapped at her, "No. My eyes are inured to ugliness, but you offend them. Get out. Go!"

She got up and went. Aiken, hunched over, writing steadily, his teeth clamped on his lip, probably hadn't heard Wolfe speak and wasn't aware that she had moved. I know I wouldn't have been, in his place.

Chapter 17

At 9:04 Saturday morning I buzzed the plant rooms on the house phone, and when Wolfe answered I told him, "It's here. I've opened it. Do I phone Cramer?"

"No. Any news?"

"No."

At 9:52 Saturday morning I buzzed the plant rooms again and told Wolfe, "Lon Cohen just phoned. About an hour ago a maid in Benedict Aiken's home found his body on the floor of his bedroom. Shot through the roof of the mouth. The gun was there on the floor. No further details at present. Do I phone Cramer?"

"Yes. Eleven o'clock."

"Certainly. If I also phoned Lon he would appreciate it. Is there any reason why I shouldn't?"

"No. The substance, not the text."

"Right."

———————

At 11:08 Saturday morning Inspector Cramer, seated in the red leather chair, looked up from the paper he held in his hand and growled at Wolfe, "You wrote this."

Wolfe, at his desk, shook his head. "Not my hand."

"Nuts. You know damn well. This word 'malefaction.' Other words. It sounds like you. You did it deliberately. You let it sound like you so I would know you wrote it. Thumbing your nose at me, telling me to kiss your ass. Oh, I know it will check with his handwriting. I wouldn't be surprised if he wrote it right here, sitting in this chair."

"Mr. Cramer." Wolfe turned a hand over. "If I granted your inference I would challenge your interpretation. I would suggest that I let it sound like me out of regard for your sensibility and respect for your talents; that I wanted to make it plain that I knew you wouldn't be gulled."

"Yeah. You can have that." He looked at the paper. "It says 'it has been made clear to me by Nero Wolfe that there is no hope of preventing disclosure.' So you had evidence. You must have had damned good evidence. What?"

Wolfe nodded. "It was impossible to prevent that question. If Mr. Aiken were still alive I would of course have to answer it. You would need the evidence and I would have to surrender it. But he's dead. I'm not a lawyer, but I have consulted one. I am not obliged to reveal evidence that is not needed and could not be used in the public interest."

"It's in the public interest to know where and when the murder was committed."

"No, sir. In the police interest, not in the public interest. It's a nice point. If you want to test it you'll have to charge me, serve a warrant on me, persuade the District Attorney to prosecute, and let a judge and jury decide. With Mr. Aiken dead and his confession in hand, I doubt if you'd get a verdict."

"So do I." Cramer folded the paper and put it in the envelope, and stuck the envelope in a pocket. "Your goddam brass." He got up. "We'll see." He turned and marched out.

At 3:47 Saturday afternoon three men and a woman were in the office with Wolfe and me. The men, in yellow chairs, were members of the board of directors of Continental Plastic Products. The woman, in the red leather chair, was Mrs. Thomas G. Yeager. In their hands were sheets of paper, copies I had typed of the document we had received in the mail that morning. Wolfe was speaking.

"No. I will not. In the terms of my engagement it was neither specified nor implied that I would report the particulars of my performance. It would serve no end to display to you the evidence with which I confronted Mr. Aiken, or to tell you how I got it. As for the result, that was determined by the situation, not by me; I merely arranged the style of the denouement. If it had been left to the police, they would certainly have discovered that room, given time; once learning about the room, they would have learned everything; and Mr. Aiken, your president, would have been, instead of the object of a brief sensation, the center of a prolonged hullabaloo. As for my fee, do you question my evaluation of my services at fifty thousand dollars?"

"No," a director said, "I don't." Another said, "We haven't questioned that." The third one grunted.

"I owe you a fee too," Mrs. Yeager said.

Wolfe shook his head. "I have your dollar; I'll keep that. I told you I don't expect a payment from two different clients for the same services." He looked up at the clock; he had his date with the orchids at four. He pushed back his chair and rose. "You may keep those copies of Mr. Aiken's statement. They're cheap at the price."

At 5:14 Saturday afternoon I was sitting in the kitchen in the basement of the house at 156 West 82nd Street. Cesar Perez was slumped in a chair. His wife was sitting straight, her shoulders back. "I'm sorry," I said, "but it can't be helped. The man who killed Maria is dead, but the police don't know it. If they did they would also know about this house and about your taking Yeager's body out of it and dumping it in the hole. So they'll be bothering you some more, but probably not for long. I'd like to go to the funeral tomorrow, but I'd better not. There will probably be a policeman there. They attend the funerals of people who have been murdered when they haven't caught the murderer. I think I've told you everything you'd want to know, but do you want to ask anything?"

He shook his head. She said, "We said we would pay you one hundred dollars."

"Forget it. We had too many clients anyway. I'll keep the dollar, and I'll also keep the keys, if you don't mind, as a souvenir. You'd better have a new lock put on the door." I left the chair and stepped to the table to get a parcel wrapped in brown paper. "This is the only thing I took from the room, a woman's umbrella. I'll return it to its owner." I shook hands, with her and then with him, and blew.

I didn't go to Eden Street. I had no overwhelming desire to see the Houghs again, or Meg Duncan offstage. On Monday I sent the umbrella and the cigarette case by messenger.

I should add a note, in case anyone reading this report takes a notion to go and take a look at the bower. You won't find it on 82nd Street. Nor will you find any of the people where I have put them. The particulars of the performance were exactly as I have reported them, but for obvious reasons I have changed names and addresses and a few other details—for instance, the title of the play Meg Duncan was starring in. It's still on and she's as good as ever; I went one night last week just to see.

If Cramer reads this and drops in to inquire, I'll tell him I made it up, including this note.

The World of
Rex Stout

Now, for the first time ever, enjoy a peek into the life of Nero Wolfe's creator, Rex Stout, courtesy of the Stout Estate. Pulled from Rex Stout's own archives, here are rarely seen, never-before-published memorabilia. Each title in "The Rex Stout Library" will offer an exclusive look into the life of the man who gave Nero Wolfe life.

Too Many Clients

Too Many Clients was called a "brain workout" by the reviewer for *Virginia Kirkus Bulletin* (now *Kirkus Reviews*) when it first appeared in 1960. The same reviewer, however, questioned whether there was too much sex(!) for some Stout fans. The paperback reprinter obviously didn't think so, and put the "sex side" right on the book's cover, in this first paperback edition from 1962.

V. KIRKUS BULLETIN
New York, N. Y.

LITERARY CLIPPING SERVICE

October 17

Stout, Rex

Viking
$2.95

TOO MANY CLIENTS

Another Nero Wolfe brain workout, with Archie Goodwin providing the leg work. They are set a multiple problem when a succession of clients - all related to the same case- come to them for help. A rich executive's love nest- the women who had keys to it- and a conflict of interest in those women provided plenty of red herrings (and considerable doubt as to who would pay the piper) before Wolfe sorted them out and came up with the answer. The sex side- while it remains on paper and in Archie's mind- may lure some readers and prove distasteful to others. (LC:60-15154)

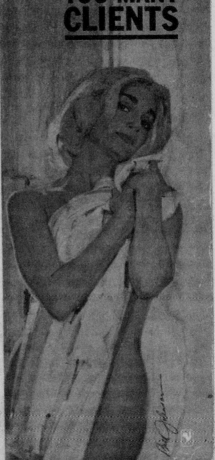

J2334 ★ ★ 40c

TOO MANY CLIENTS

A NERO WOLFE MYSTERY

REX STOUT